CW01457744

THE COLOUR OF HOPE

By Danielle Steel

The Colour of Hope • The Portrait • For Richer for Poorer • A Mother's Love
A Mind of Her Own • Far from Home • Never Say Never • Trial by Fire • Triangle
Joy • Resurrection • Only the Brave • Never Too Late • Upside Down
The Ball at Versailles • Second Act • Happiness • Palazzo • The Wedding Planner
Worthy Opponents • Without a Trace • The Whittiers • The High Notes • The Challenge
Suspects • Beautiful • High Stakes • Invisible • Flying Angels • The Butler • Complications
Nine Lives • Finding Ashley • The Affair • Neighbours • All That Glitters • Royal
Daddy's Girls • The Wedding Dress • The Numbers Game • Moral Compass • Spy
Child's Play • The Dark Side • Lost and Found • Blessing in Disguise • Silent Night
Turning Point • Beauchamp Hall • In His Father's Footsteps • The Good Fight • The Cast
Accidental Heroes • Fall from Grace • Past Perfect • Fairytale • The Right Time
The Duchess • Against All Odds • Dangerous Games • The Mistress • The Award
Rushing Waters • Magic • The Apartment • Property of a Noblewoman • Blue
Precious Gifts • Undercover • Country • Prodigal Son • Pegasus • A Perfect Life
Power Play • Winners • First Sight • Until the End of Time • The Sins of the Mother
Friends Forever • Betrayal • Hotel Vendôme • Happy Birthday • 44 Charles Street • Legacy
Family Ties • Big Girl • Southern Lights • Matters of the Heart • One Day at a Time
A Good Woman • Rogue • Honor Thyself • Amazing Grace • Bungalow 2 • Sisters
H.R.H. • Coming Out • The House • Toxic Bachelors • Miracle • Impossible • Echoes
Second Chance • Ransom • Safe Harbour • Johnny Angel • Dating Game
Answered Prayers • Sunset in St. Tropez • The Cottage • The Kiss • Leap of Faith
Lone Eagle • Journey • The House on Hope Street • The Wedding • Irresistible Forces
Granny Dan • Bittersweet • Mirror Image • The Klone and I • The Long Road Home
The Ghost • Special Delivery • The Ranch • Silent Honor • Malice • Five Days in Paris
Lightning • Wings • The Gift • Accident • Vanished • Mixed Blessings • Jewels
No Greater Love • Heartbeat • Message from Nam • Daddy • Star • Zoya • Kaleidoscope
Fine Things • Wanderlust • Secrets • Family Album • Full Circle • Changes
Thurston House • Crossings • Once in a Lifetime • A Perfect Stranger • Remembrance
Palomino • Love: *Poems* • The Ring • Loving • To Love Again • Summer's End
Season of Passion • The Promise • Now and Forever • Passion's Promise • Going Home

Nonfiction

Expect a Miracle
Pure Joy: *The Dogs We Love*
A Gift of Hope: *Helping the Homeless*
His Bright Light: *The Story of Nick Traina*

For Children

Pretty Minnie in Hollywood
Pretty Minnie in Paris

Danielle Steel

THE COLOUR OF HOPE

MACMILLAN

First published 2025 by Delacorte Press
an imprint of Random House
a division of Penguin Random House LLC, New York

First published in the UK 2025 by Macmillan
an imprint of Pan Macmillan
The Smithson, 6 Briset Street, London EC1M 5NR
EU representative: Macmillan Publishers Ireland Limited, 1st Floor,
The Liffey Trust Centre, 117–126 Sheriff Street Upper,
Dublin 1 D01 YC43
Associated companies throughout the world

ISBN 978-1-5290-8606-5 HB
ISBN 978-1-5290-8607-2 TPB

Copyright © Danielle Steel 2025

The right of Danielle Steel to be identified as the
author of this work has been asserted in accordance
with the Copyright, Designs and Patents Act 1988.

All rights reserved. No part of this publication may be reproduced,
stored in a retrieval system, or transmitted, in any form, or by any means
(including, without limitation, electronic, mechanical, photocopying, recording
or otherwise) without the prior written permission of the publisher.

Pan Macmillan does not have any control over, or any responsibility for,
any author or third-party websites (including, without limitation, URLs,
emails and QR codes) referred to in or on this book.

1 3 5 7 9 8 6 4 2

A CIP catalogue record for this book is available from the British Library.

Typeset in Charter ITC by Palimpsest Book Production Ltd, Falkirk, Stirlingshire
Printed and bound in the UK using 100% Renewable Electricity by CPI Group (UK) Ltd

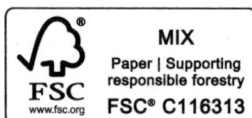

MIX
Paper | Supporting
responsible forestry
FSC® C116313
FSC
www.fsc.org

This book is sold subject to the condition that it shall not, by way of
trade or otherwise, be lent, hired out, or otherwise circulated without
the publisher's prior consent in any form of binding or cover other than
that in which it is published and without a similar condition including
this condition being imposed on the subsequent purchaser. The publisher does not
authorize the use or reproduction of any part of this book in any manner for the
purpose of training artificial intelligence technologies or systems. The publisher
expressly reserves this book from the Text and Data Mining exception in accordance
with Article 4(3) of the European Union Digital Single Market Directive 2019/790.

Visit **www.panmacmillan.com** to read more
about all our books and to buy them.

To my beloved children,
Beatrix, Trevor, Todd, Nick, Samantha,
Victoria, Vanessa, Maxx, and Zara,

May the losses in your lives be small ones,
but large or small, stay open to life,
and embrace the love and surprises
that life bestows on you, unexpected,
greater than you could imagine.

After loss, love and happiness come again.
Always paint your life the color of hope.
Be kind to each other, and always know
that I love you with all my heart and soul,

Mommy / d.s.

No matter how wounded you are,
you should still play the game.

—MORTON L. JANKLOW, literary agent

THE COLOUR OF HOPE

Chapter 1

Sabrina Thompson stood looking around the living room of her Malibu home, momentarily at a loss. It was a spectacular modern house. Everything was white and open and airy. She and her husband had loved the location and the view of the beach and the ocean. Malcolm had bought it from a famous Hollywood producer for a fortune. They had gutted it and almost completely redesigned it as their romantic weekend getaway, with the eventual intention of using it as their retirement home, their home base from which to travel. Malcolm had had an epiphany three years before when he turned fifty and their youngest child, Colette, "Coco," left for college in New York, at Parsons School of Design, her lifetime dream. He decided to retire in five years, at fifty-five. They bought the Malibu house as their future home, and planned to sell their enormous Bel Air house after he retired, and live in Malibu between trips. They had already put Bel Air on the market at an enormous price and expected it to take a few years to sell. They weren't in a hurry since he hadn't retired yet. It had taken them two years to achieve the look they wanted in Malibu, and they started spending weekends there as soon as the construction and decorating was finished.

They had been empty nesters now for four years. Their oldest child, Justin, had gone to Yale, as Sabrina had. She had majored in Fine Arts, and Justin majored in business and economics and was now doing graduate studies at the London School of Economics for a master's in Economics and Management. He was twenty-five. Elizabeth, "Lizzie," their second child, had gone to Princeton, then straight to law school at Columbia when she graduated. She was now in her third and final year at twenty-four. Coco had graduated from Parsons six months earlier and was doing an internship at Prada in Milan and loving it.

Sabrina was the daughter of Hollywood royalty. Her father was a famous producer, who had made some of the biggest movies in the industry, and her mother had been a promising young starlet, when they met and fell in love. She had married him at twenty-three, and abandoned her career immediately. He was eighteen years older, and she had been a wife and mother for the rest of her life, and had no regrets about her career. They had been wonderful parents and doted on Sabrina, their only child. Sabrina had followed in her mother's footsteps and married young at twenty-two. She was a talented artist, and had given up her career aspirations too, to raise her and Malcolm's three children.

She felt lost at first when the children left for college, and Malcolm had encouraged her to open the art gallery she had always dreamed of. She had opened it in a beautiful space on Melrose Place in L.A., and had fun with it. She treated the artists she represented like her children, and loved their work. She sold their paintings and sculptures at moderate prices to make the work accessible and help advance their careers. It was a labor of love more than a job and she was having a great time with it. She'd owned it for four years, and often traveled to art fairs to look for new artists. She was a talented muralist herself, but only used her talent now for their own homes and select friends. She loved being Malcolm's wife and her children's mother. She was a quiet, private person, and had no thirst for celebrity or fame. All doors would have been open to her if she had wanted a career as an actress, but she had no interest in that whatsoever. Her only career aspirations had ever been as an artist, but she was focused now only on the work of the artists she represented, not her own.

Malcolm had come to L.A. from New York to attend USC. He was also an only child, and after college he had gotten a job at a television network in L.A., where he had risen through the ranks, with no help from his powerful father-in-law. He built his career on his own merits. He was twenty-seven when he married Sabrina, and they had three babies in the first three years. At forty he had become the head of the network, and he was happy with the decision he made at fifty to retire at fifty-five. He thought that another five years in a high-powered, ruthlessly demanding job he nonetheless enjoyed would be enough. He wasn't power-hungry, he enjoyed what he did and was good at it. But he wanted to be free to enjoy life with Sabrina while they were young enough to do so. One of their goals for "after network television" was to buy an apartment in Paris and spend time there too.

The beautiful big home in Bel Air seemed cavernous without the children once they left. Sabrina and Malcolm didn't need a house that size. It had made perfect sense when their children were young and it was constantly filled with other kids coming and going and spending weekends. They had the house where all their children's friends wanted to hang out, which they had set up intentionally so that they could keep a good eye on their kids, know their friends, guide them gently, and see what was going on. But once their children left, the house felt sad to both of them. It had served its purpose, and when the house they had redesigned in Malibu was ready, after two years of construction, they put the Bel Air house on the market, after discussing it with their children, none of whom planned to ever live in L.A. again. The fashion world would take Coco to Paris, New York, or Milan. Lizzie had fallen in love with New York, and wanted to pass the bar and work for a law firm there when she graduated from law school, and Justin was enthralled with London, and wanted to spend the early years of his career in Europe for the international finance experience he'd get there.

Even if any of them decided to come back to L.A. eventually, they wouldn't want to live at home. So Malcolm and Sabrina put their family home on the market at a very hefty price. They were in no rush, and they were having fun together in a more manageable house at the beach on the weekends. It was their love nest, and better suited to a couple with grown children. They didn't need a big staff to run it. They used a cleaning service, and liked being alone on the weekends. Each of the children had a bedroom, and there were two additional guest rooms. The Malibu house was a blank page. They had no history there, no memories, the way they did in Bel Air, of their children's childhoods and the happy years they had spent there. The house in

Malibu felt new and fresh. It was better suited to their life of the future. Bel Air was the symbol of the past, and didn't suit the life they were planning after Malcolm retired. They wanted to be free to roam the world.

Malcolm and Sabrina were one of those couples who had done everything right. They had married the right people and were still in love twenty-six years later, and there had been no marital slips or regrets. They had good children, and had brought them up with strong family values and encouraged them to pursue their dreams, just as Malcolm had encouraged Sabrina to pursue hers with the art gallery she loved owning once the kids were gone. She was serious about it and dedicated to her artists. She worked closely with the gallery manager she had hired, Hallie Brooks, who was a skilled artist too, and had a business degree from UCLA. Sabrina and Hallie were good friends and worked well together.

And Malcolm had succeeded admirably at his career. He had made a very respectable fortune, was a responsible person, a good husband and father. He and Sabrina had both lost their parents in the course of their marriage, and Sabrina had her own money, inherited from her parents. Malcolm's parents had been more modest, and he had made his own fortune and was generous with it. They had a warm circle of friends, but were closest to each other, unusually so.

Sabrina was intelligent, and Malcolm often discussed his hard decisions with her, and respected her opinions and advice. She felt certain that she was married to the best man on the planet and had never looked at another man with interest, although she was beautiful, tall, thin, and blonde, and many of Malcolm's friends envied him. Malcolm and Sabrina were people of integrity, good parents, respected in their community and admired as a couple, even looked upon with envy by some. Malcolm always operated on the theory that good things happened to good people, and he was grateful for what they shared. He didn't take it for granted. They loved each other deeply and made a conscious effort to do the right thing and honor their word, and it seemed only fair that a steady stream of good things had happened to them in their twenty-six years together. No accidents or tragedies had occurred professionally or personally. They were sad to have lost their parents, but they were of an appropriate age and had led good lives.

A year before, Sabrina and Malcolm had gone to Paris to celebrate New Year's when their children left after Christmas with their own plans. They always stayed at the Ritz in Paris, and had a favorite suite that felt like home to them. There were adjacent rooms for the children when they went as a family, which they did in the summer when they spent a week together at their favorite hotel in the south of France. The children never missed it. But the New Year's trip to Paris was a romantic tryst for Malcolm and Sabrina.

Sabrina was startled when Malcolm tripped and twisted his ankle on the front steps of the Ritz. He was very athletic, played a lot of tennis, and had never done that before. He dropped a thermos of coffee at breakfast a few days later, when helping himself to a second cup, and a bottle of champagne when pouring a glass for each of them on New Year's Day. She had an uneasy feeling about it. There were no other mishaps on the trip, but he fell at the Bel Air house one afternoon at the pool. She nagged him to go to the doctor after that, and he brushed it off. It was a busy time in the office, and he felt fine.

It took two more minor incidents in February, when she noticed he had difficulty holding a pen when he was signing something, and his speech seemed slurred one morning, which worried him too. He finally saw the doctor and had a battery of tests. Sabrina worried that he might be having small strokes, which could account for his falling, and his loosening grip and dropping things. He was only fifty-three years old, and they were two years away from his retirement plan. But he had a high-pressure job and it took a toll.

Malcolm's doctor was thorough, ordering more exams and MRIs, and sending him to a series of specialists. He had electrodiagnostic tests, including electromyography and a study of nerve conduction velocity, extensive blood studies, hormones, thyroid and parathyroid studies, X-rays, another MRI, a spinal tap, a myelogram, a nerve biopsy, and a neurological exam. The doctors left no stone unturned. Neither Malcolm nor Sabrina was prepared for the diagnosis that resulted from the extensive tests.

Malcolm's primary physician delivered the news as gently as he could. Malcolm had amyotrophic lateral sclerosis, more commonly known as ALS, or Lou Gehrig's disease. Neither Malcolm nor Sabrina admitted it to each other, but they recognized it was a death sentence, with an agonizing descent into hell ahead. They had no idea how or why he had gotten it, and there was no cure. It was a degenerative disease which would affect his motor skills. Eventually his nerve cells would be destroyed, and he would no longer be able to speak, swallow, or breathe. The end would come on a ventilator, with his mind still intact. The average length of survival was three years. Dr. Farber said that some people lived for five or ten years with ALS, and a rare five percent lived for twenty, which was something to hope for. And Malcolm might have periods of "arrests" or "reversals" when the disease would stop advancing, or improve for a year or longer, which happened in one percent of cases. The odds were not in Malcolm's favor, even applying his theory that good things happened to good people, which he certainly was. But for the first time he and Sabrina had to face the fact that bad things happened too. Even very bad things sometimes, and this was one.

They were both in shock when they got the diagnosis. Sabrina drove them home. Malcolm no longer felt comfortable driving, and as soon as they got home they both burst into sobs and clung to each other. It was the worst nightmare either of them could imagine, and his motor skills were already affected. There was no way of telling how long he would live, and in what condition, whether or not he would have an arrest or reversal, or how fast the disease would move, or if he would be one of the lucky one or five percent who could live ten or twenty years. In twenty years, he'd be seventy-three, still too young to die.

Malcolm went back to work the day after the diagnosis, and Sabrina spent the day at home crying. Nothing worse could have happened, except if he had died suddenly. But he was facing an agonizing end. He was very brave about it, and more worried about Sabrina than himself.

The disease was merciless, and its advance relentless. By the end of February, he could no longer walk, was in a wheelchair, and had lost the use of his hands. He had explained the situation confidentially to the chairman of the network, who was heartbroken for him. The diagnosis and prognosis were so cruel. Malcolm said that he would be retiring imminently, and made strong suggestions for his successor. The governing board was devastated.

Malcolm and Sabrina asked the children to come home for the weekend, and told them the news. They were as shocked and heartbroken as their parents, and they tried to be positive that he would be one of the lucky ones. But Malcolm's luck had run out, after a perfect record until then. It was a tearful weekend with the children, who tried valiantly to be brave for their parents' sake, and gave vent to their worst fears when the three of them were alone late at night.

Malcolm gave his resignation to the network at the beginning of March. His speech was difficult to understand, and failed entirely within a month. He used a computer he could manage, and then an iPad, to communicate with Sabrina and his doctors. The disease advanced at a galloping rate. Sabrina was with him every instant. She hired nurses in April to help move him, but she cared for him herself with infinite love and tenderness. He could still breathe and was spared the ventilator until his final days.

The children came home in May and spent the last three weeks with their father. They were all with him, quietly around his bed, touching him, as he looked at them gratefully and with regret, and died in Sabrina's arms in June.

The end had not been painful but it was infinitely sad, and the hardest thing any of them had ever lived through, and the most agonizingly adult experience his children would ever have to face.

One of the last things Malcolm had written to Sabrina on the iPad was that he wanted her to buy an apartment or a house in Paris. It was the last thing on her mind in his final hours. Coco had seen what he wrote, and smiled. Their father had been a remarkable man—even at death's door, he thought of everyone but himself.

The network offered whatever help they could, but there was nothing they could do. Sabrina's gallery manager helped her make the funeral arrangements, and her children did what they could to support their mother and each other. She was dignified and strong for them. They left after the funeral, brokenhearted, but Lizzie and Justin had to go back to school, and Coco had to get back to work in Milan. Their schools and Prada had been compassionate about their being absent for their father's final days, but they couldn't extend it any longer. Sabrina had to manage on her own after they left. She felt paralyzed with grief and could barely get out of bed. Malcolm had lived four months after the diagnosis and degenerated at lightning speed. It was a mercy for him but intolerably painful for her. She couldn't imagine her life without him. She hadn't been to the gallery in two months, and had no desire to go there at all. Hallie, the gallery manager, took care of everything, and came by the house to check on her. She could tell that Sabrina wasn't eating. She had lost a shocking amount of weight by July, and the family canceled their summer trip to the south of France. No one was in the mood for it. The children came home for a week in August, and it was a very dark time. They were all worried about their mother when they left, but they couldn't stay. They had lives and obligations in other cities. Sabrina tried to put a good face on it, but the truth was easily visible in how thin she was.

At the end of August, she had a jolt she didn't expect. The Bel Air house was still on the market, which she had forgotten about completely. She had stopped all realtor visits while Malcolm was ill, and she hadn't started them again yet. And suddenly, she had a serious offer. The last thing she wanted was to sell the house right now. They had stayed at the Bel Air house while Malcolm was ill. It was closer to the hospital and worked better with the nurses and the help they needed. And she hadn't been back to Malibu since Malcolm died. She felt closer to him in Bel Air. She had Hallie decline the offer, and the potential buyer raised it significantly. It was an offer she couldn't ignore, and she called the children for their advice. She felt sentimental about the house, especially with Malcolm having just died there. But all three children agreed that she would bury herself alive in the Bel Air home, and advised her to sell it. "What would Dad want you to do?" Lizzie asked her, knowing the response. Malcolm had wanted to sell it before, and he was an astute businessman who wouldn't let an offer like that go by. The prospective buyer was one of the biggest director/producers in Hollywood and had admired the house for years, had been there before and knew it well, and was hoping that Sabrina would sell it to him with Malcolm gone.

"He'd tell me to sell," Sabrina said to Lizzie with a sigh. Financially, it was the right thing to do, although she didn't need the money. She had her own, and Malcolm had left her half of his very comfortable fortune, and divided the other half into thirds for the children. They'd been handsomely provided for.

After several days of hard reflection, Sabrina accepted their offer. The buyer was paying almost double their asking price, all cash, and wanted a sixty-day closing.

Feeling like a robot, she put most of the contents in storage for the children, and moved what she needed to Malibu in October. She hadn't been there in months.

She had moved to Malibu as her only home now two months before, and now she looked around the living room, trying to decide where to put the Christmas tree for their first Christmas without Malcolm, and the first in Malibu. The house looked like a breath of summer, light and open and airy, all decorated in white. She had been happy there with Malcolm, but it didn't look like Christmas or feel like it as she picked a place for the tree in the living room, near the white marble Italian fireplace. She had brought all their Christmas decorations from Bel Air. They would look strange in this sleek, ultracontemporary house, and she sorted through them, picking the ones she knew the children loved most, and those that would look the best in the house. It took her several days to do the tree alone, and she had Hallie help her string tiny lights in the hedges and small trees around the house and on the patio. She couldn't stop crying while she did it, and Hallie felt terrible for her.

"Why don't you let me do it?" Hallie begged, but Sabrina wouldn't let her. She wanted to do it with her. She still missed the Bel Air house, and their happy memories there. But she knew selling had been the right thing to do. She couldn't hang on to the past, and she and Malcolm had made the decision a year before to sell it. The timing was just hard, right after Malcolm's death. She was trying to be brave about it. She stood back and looked at the Christmas tree when they finished the lights and she smiled. It was the first smile Hallie had seen from her in six months, since June. And there had been few smiles in the months before that while Malcolm deteriorated day by day and was dying.

"It looks nice," Sabrina said, satisfied.

"It looks beautiful," Hallie said to her. She knew that Sabrina had bought gifts for her children, although fewer than usual. She didn't have the heart or the energy to shop. But she had bought small, thoughtful gifts for all fifteen of her artists, and was having Hallie give them a Christmas party at the gallery, with a buffet dinner, though she wasn't going to attend herself. She was in deep mourning for the only man she had ever loved. She was forty-eight years old and she felt as dead as he was. She couldn't envision a future or a life without him.

When they finished hanging the lights, Hallie ordered food for them. There was nothing in the fridge to make a meal of, and when they sat down to eat, Sabrina picked at her dinner, and barely ate enough to feed a child. She couldn't eat or sleep without Malcolm. She still couldn't absorb what had happened. It went against everything they had both believed. Until then, they had led a charmed life. Now the dream was over.

Their friends had been calling her since June, and she sent messages to thank them for their calls. There was no one she wanted to talk to. Malcolm had been her best friend and confidant, the perfect partner for their life's adventure. She felt as though she had lost her voice and her spirit. She tried to sound upbeat for the children when they called, as she didn't want to worry them, but they knew her better. She knew she just had to get through it day by day, but so far she didn't feel any better than she had on the day he died. Hallie wondered how long it would take, and so did her children. Their parents had been so close, so happy, and so much a part of each other's lives that Sabrina felt as though someone had torn her limbs off, or carved out her heart with a knife. A life without him was inconceivable, but it was what she had to face now. He was never coming back. The thought of it made her feel faint sometimes.

Hallie brought her up to date on the gallery over dinner, and then she left. The lights they'd put on the trees in the patio were twinkling brightly when she drove away, and the tree in the living room looked beautiful for the children. Sabrina wasn't going to let them down. She knew she had to make the best of it for them. She had to do it for Malcolm, and for her children, but she couldn't imagine Christmas without him, or any other day of the year. He had taken her heart and soul with him, and she felt like an empty shell. She felt like she had no real home now, no solid ground under her feet. He had been her rock, her foundation, her joy, her bright blue sky, the sun that lit her world. And it was a very dark world now without him. The only thing she had to look forward to was Christmas with her children. They were staying for five days, and then she would be alone again. They wanted to be back in their own cities to celebrate New Year's with their friends. And Sabrina knew that after they left, the life ahead of her would be a long lonely road to eternity without Malcolm. She couldn't even imagine it, any more than she could have imagined the past six months, or the year she had just been through.

She turned off the lights in the living room, and left the tree lit for a minute. It looked beautiful, and was picture-perfect. But Christmas without Malcolm in the house that had been their weekend love nest was unthinkable. She clicked the remote control to turn off the tree, and walked up the stairs in the dark to her bedroom for another sleep-less night without him.

Chapter 2

The house looked perfect when the children arrived. The tree was lit, hung with their familiar decorations. Sabrina had brought many of their favorite paintings with her from Bel Air, and had put a number of them in storage for the children to have later when they had proper homes, not just small student apartments. None of the children were established yet, and two were still in school. They were only in their twenties, and she and Malcolm had bought many important paintings they loved. Sabrina had hung several of his favorites in their bedroom when she moved. Just seeing them was a warm reminder of him. It was bittersweet when she woke up in the morning after a few hours' sleep, glanced at the paintings, and remembered when they'd bought them and how much he loved them.

She'd hung some bright happy paintings from her gallery in the living room when they decorated the house. Malcolm had liked them too. She had intended to do a mural in the dining room and hadn't gotten around to it yet. She had time to do it now, but she didn't have the heart. Without Malcolm there to see it, it seemed irrelevant, and she didn't plan to entertain without him.

The children were arriving that afternoon. Coco had flown to New York from Milan the night before and stayed with Lizzie. They were flying to L.A. together that afternoon. Justin was taking a direct flight from London and would be arriving an hour after his sisters. By dinnertime the house would be full of laughter and noise, with the music the children played drifting from their rooms. Sabrina was excited. For the first time in months she had something to look forward to.

"How do you think Mom is doing?" Coco asked her older sister as the plane took off from New York. She worried about her mother, but it was hard to make the time difference work to call her. Coco worked long hours in Milan and it was always the wrong time to call when she got home, or she fell asleep, exhausted, and forgot, or she was too late for work in the morning to call her mother.

"I don't know," Lizzie answered. "She says she's fine, but

she doesn't sound great. And Hallie told me she hasn't been to the gallery in months. I don't know what she does all day. Her life is pretty empty without Dad, especially with none of us at home. Her whole life revolved around him." Coco nodded, pensively. She felt guilty about it at times, but it was the life Sabrina had chosen, to be a full-time wife. She'd been busy with the gallery for the past few years, but if she wasn't going there, and their father was gone, she had nothing to do, except think about him.

"We'll know how she is when we see her," Coco said quietly. "There's not much we can do at a distance." Coco was as fair as her mother, though not as tall. And Lizzie had dark hair and looked more like their father. Justin was the image of Malcolm in his youth. Coco was as thin as the models she worked with at Prada, while Lizzie had a slightly fuller figure. They were both beautiful young women, and several men had noticed them as they got on the plane. Coco had a decidedly fashionable European look, with a big battered vintage Hermès alligator hand-bag. She was wearing black jeans and a black sweater with a synthetic leopard-printed coat that looked real, her blonde hair pulled back sleekly, and a big gold bracelet on her arm that their mother had given her for Christmas the year before. Lizzie was wearing jeans, a navy blue down jacket, and sneakers, and looked like the student she was. They were looking forward to being all together. They hadn't been home since their father's funeral, although they tried to call their mother every few days. It was easier for Lizzie from New York. Coco texted her every day, and Justin texted her a few times a week, when he thought of it.

They chatted during the meal, and Lizzie watched a movie when Coco fell asleep. She had told her about the job in Milan. She was loving it and being in Europe. She had been to Paris twice on weekends when she wasn't working, and went to Rome frequently with friends. Neither of them had had time to visit Justin in London. He had an English girlfriend now, Arabella, whom none of them had met, although they had FaceTimed with them. He had met her at school the year before and she had a job now at the London office of Goldman Sachs. They were both pursuing careers in finance, and Justin had told them that Arabella's father was in the House of Lords and an earl, and Arabella was Lady Arabella, although she didn't use her title. She came from a distinguished family. The three siblings stayed in close touch and texted each other frequently, even more so now since their father had died. It had been a hard blow for all of them, and they were worried about how hard the holidays would be without him.

"It's going to be weird not seeing Dad when we go home," Coco said sadly when she woke up when they landed. It had just hit her again that he wouldn't be there.

"It would have been harder in Bel Air," Lizzie said. There were too many memories in their old house. At least a different location might help. They thought it would be better for their mother too.

At the aiport, they rented a car that they were going to share. None of them kept cars in L.A. anymore. They didn't spend enough time there to use them. They only got to L.A. once or twice a year now. Lizzie was swamped in her last year of law school, and L.A. was a long way for Coco from Milan. They were just glad they would have Christmas together.

Lizzie drove to Malibu from the airport, and they chatted on the way. They had always gotten along well. They were only two years apart. There had never been any rivalry between them. Their parents had encouraged kindness and close family ties. They got along well with their brother too. "I hope Arabella doesn't try to change that," Lizzie said as they drove home. She wasn't coming to L.A. with Justin. She was going to be with her own family for the holidays at their country home. Arabella had two sisters and a brother of her own, and was the youngest, she had told them on the phone. She seemed like a nice girl and Justin said she was very bright, and had landed a very good job. She was twenty-six, a year older than Justin.

The house in Malibu was an hour from the airport in afternoon traffic, but the time went quickly as the sisters chatted, and then they saw the gates to their new family home. They'd been there before but not often, since their parents liked to go there alone, and the children teased them about it. Malcolm and Sabrina had been careful over the years to set time aside for each other. It annoyed the children at times, but had kept their relationship solid and strong.

"It used to bother me as a kid that they were still so romantic. Now I hope I have a relationship like theirs one day," Lizzie said, as she pressed a buzzer and the gates swung open and they drove in.

"I think it's pretty rare," Coco said, thinking about her parents. "I've been in Italy for six months, and I've only had one date, and he was a jerk. All the guys I meet are gay. Meeting straight guys in fashion isn't easy," she commented, as they rolled up the driveway. You couldn't see the house from the gate.

"All the guys I meet are nerds," Lizzie said with a laugh. "And no one has time to date. We've either got papers to turn in or exams. It's pretty intense. I've got a paper to do over Christmas. I think it's going to be rough until we graduate in May."

"I have to start work on our February show as soon as I go back," Coco said, as the house came into view. It was an elegant two-story home on a large piece of land, which was rare in Malibu and why the property had been so expensive. Their mother was waiting in the driveway for them, in white jeans, a big white sweater, a silver down jacket, and silver Chanel ballerinas. She was smiling in anticipation, and her hair was pulled back in a ponytail like Coco's. "She looks good," Coco said, checking out her outfit. Sabrina always looked chic and pulled together, even in casual clothes.

"No, she doesn't," Lizzie said in a soft voice. "Don't look at the outfit. Look at her face. She looks ravaged, she's lost weight, and she's not wearing makeup." When Coco looked closer she saw that her sister was right, and their mother had dark circles under her eyes she hadn't bothered to cover. She was standing next to the car by then, and as soon as Lizzie turned off the engine, Coco jumped out of the car and hugged her mother tight. Even in the down jacket, she could tell that Sabrina was skin and bones. But she looked genuinely thrilled to see her daughters, and she hugged Lizzie an instant after Coco. The three of them walked to the patio and the girls could see the lights in the trees.

"The trees look so pretty, Mom," Lizzie said, admiring what she'd done. "Did someone do that for you?"

"I did it with Hallie." Sabrina laughed, looking at both her daughters. They looked beautiful and fresh and young. They were like a breath of air. They glanced around at the touches she had added since they'd last been there. They hadn't been to Malibu in months and had stayed in Bel Air during their father's final weeks.

Sabrina had brought their outdoor furniture from Bel Air. The Malibu house had a huge pool, and a tennis court. And the sisters knew that their father kept his vintage sailboat at the beach club. They wondered what their mother had done with it, but neither of them wanted to ask. Malcolm had been crazy about his boat, the *Sabrina Fair*. The original film with Humphrey Bogart and Audrey Hepburn had been one of his and Sabrina's favorite movies. It was made long before they were born but they loved it anyway. Malcolm was a big Humphrey Bogart fan, Sabrina loved Audrey Hepburn, and they both loved classic films. They tried to get their children interested in them, but never succeeded, although once in a while Coco watched them as part of her fashion research, to see the clothes. She agreed with her mother about Audrey Hepburn. She was the chicest woman who had ever lived. The children did enjoy watching their grandfather's films. He was a Hollywood legend and had made some great movies. They loved watching their grandmother in her early movies, before she married and gave up acting to be a wife. And it always struck them how much their mother looked like her, and Coco too.

Lizzie went to get the bags out of the car. She had brought one very compact suitcase, and Coco had brought two big ones. They'd each brought something nice to wear on Christmas and casual clothes for the rest of their stay. They had no plans and didn't want to make dates to see their old friends until they saw what kind of shape their mother was in. It didn't seem to be the right year for them to be socializing, with their father so recently deceased. And a number of their school friends had moved away to other cities to find jobs after college. Several were in New York, and Lizzie saw them when she had time, which wasn't often because of law school.

A gardener working outside the house carried the bags upstairs for them, and Sabrina thanked him with a warm smile and a few words. Then he came downstairs and went back to working outside. Their old housekeeper from the Bel Air house had semiretired, and was coming two or three times a week to check on the cleaning service and to buy groceries for Sabrina. Otherwise, she knew, Sabrina wouldn't eat.

They walked into the house together, and the girls smiled when they saw the tree. They recognized their favorite decorations and Christmas balls immediately and thanked their mother for bringing them to the new house. It was a thoughtful gesture they appreciated. She was always attentive to them, as she had been to their father. They followed her into the kitchen where she made tea for them, and they sat at the kitchen table for a few minutes and talked about nothing special, while the girls tried to get a feeling for how Sabrina was. The circles under her eyes told their own tale. She looked tired, and there was a look of despair in her eyes that Lizzie didn't like, while Coco admired her silver shoes.

When they finished the tea, both girls went upstairs to freshen up, and Coco wandered into Lizzie's bedroom and closed the door. "Mom looks so tired and she's so thin," Coco said, worried about her. She could see now why Lizzie was concerned. The soundtrack seemed okay, and Sabrina sounded lively, but the picture wasn't good when you looked closely.

"She probably isn't sleeping, or eating," Lizzie said. "She must sit around thinking about Dad all day. Her life must be pretty dismal without him, and lonely." They both felt sorry for her. They missed their father too, but they had lives and school and jobs and friends, and interactions with other people. Sabrina had nothing except memories and a silent house. It made her daughters sad for her. Being there brought it all into sharper focus. But she was putting on a good front for them.

Lizzie and Coco sat on the patio with her when they came back downstairs. There was a stack of blankets on a chair near them, which they didn't need in the daytime. There were large pool towels too, in case anyone wanted to swim, which the girls didn't.

Half an hour later, Justin arrived. His plane had been on time, and he was as happy to see the girls as they were to see him. The three of them hugged and then he hugged his mother. He was delighted to see all of them, and he FaceTimed Arabella to tell her he had arrived safely. It was the first time Sabrina had seen her. She was a very pretty young blonde woman with an aristocratic look.

They had dinner together that night, having ordered takeout from Giorgio Baldi in Santa Monica. It took a long time to arrive, but they had a delicious meal. Then Justin made a fire in the white marble and glass fireplace and they shared a bottle of wine their mother poured for them. Lizzie laughed, remembering all the times she had gotten in trouble in her teens. Coco had been easier and rarely balked at her parents' rules. Lizzie had been bolder and more argumentative. Lizzie had reminded Justin of when he had stolen their father's car from the garage and taken it for a spin, without a license, when he was fifteen.

"And I got a flat tire," he added sheepishly, "and had to call Dad for help. He didn't even know the car was gone until I called him. I was grounded for a month." Their parents had been more lenient with Coco, because she was younger and Sabrina said they were "broken in" by then.

It was hard for Sabrina to believe how quickly the years had flown. Even the girls were aware of it. It all seemed so far away, and what had been dramatic then, and so serious, seemed funny now. They had grown up to be decent people. Sabrina was proud of them.

They went for a walk on the beach the next day, all four of them. They were a cohesive little unit and every time she saw them together, Sabrina was acutely aware that someone was missing. It was constantly apparent and she still had the feeling that Malcolm would walk in at any minute and tell them it was all a joke. But it wasn't. It was deadly serious, he was gone, and never coming back. She had to make her peace with it, but she still didn't see how. She loved being with her children, but it made her miss her husband more. He belonged with them, still making plans for his retirement, so they could spend more time together, and now that time would never come.

They followed all their usual traditions, which was comforting. Sabrina said grace at the beginning of the meal, as she always did on holidays. Malcolm had left that to her.

They played games after dinner, Clue and charades and card games. Malcolm had liked to play liar's dice with them, but Sabrina hadn't brought the dice out. It was too sharp a reminder of their father. It had been his favorite game, and they were all good at it. But he had been the grand master of the liar's dice games.

The evening ended well, and in the morning, they exchanged their gifts and had a late breakfast in pajamas. Sabrina had hired caterers to prepare their Christmas dinner, and she was relieved the day after when it was over. They had made it through Christmas without Malcolm, and Sabrina was grateful she and her children had been together. Being in Malibu had made it easier for all of them, since they had never celebrated Christmas with him there.

"So what are your plans now, Mom?" Lizzie asked her mother gingerly as they were putting the breakfast dishes in the dishwasher on the twenty-sixth. Justin and Coco had gone to play tennis at the tennis court on the property. Justin had said he was going surfing that afternoon. Sabrina had brought his wetsuit from Bel Air. It was in his room.

"I don't have any plans," Sabrina said quietly. How could she make plans without Malcolm? It seemed like a sacrilege, to make plans and have fun without him. It seemed disrespectful. And she didn't have the energy or desire to plan anything. After the children left, she was going to sink back into the quicksand of her solitude again. It wasn't a plan, it was inevitable, with nothing to look forward to.

Lizzie had been trying to think of ways to pull her mother out of her slump. Sabrina covered it well for them, but Lizzie could sense how unhappy and lifeless she was under her pretense to them of being "fine."

"I've been thinking about something, Mom," she said cautiously, not sure how her mother would respond. "I remembered how much Dad wanted you to get an apartment in Paris. He talked about it again right before the end. It meant a lot to him. You should think about that now, to honor his memory. It was what he wanted for you." Lizzie was hoping that by framing it as her father's dying wish, her mother might be more receptive to the idea. She expected her to balk at first, and she did.

"What would I do with an apartment in Paris now?" Sabrina looked shocked. "It was for both of us, and he wouldn't be there to share it with me. It makes no sense."

"It makes a lot of sense. What are you going to do? You can't just sit and stare at the ocean and wish he was here. He wouldn't want you to do that, Mom. That's why he reminded you about the apartment in Paris. He *wanted* that for you. Not just to share with him. For *you*. And we'd all like that too. None of us can be here with you, and we don't want you unhappy here alone. I know you're sad, and you have a right to be. You and Dad had a fantastic marriage, the best I've ever seen, and I can only imagine how awful you feel right now. But he wanted something special for you, to make you happy, as a last gift from him. You'd be honoring his wishes if you found a great place in Paris and spent some time there." She said it as gently as she could, hoping not to scare her off, and that she'd warm to the idea.

"I'd be there alone too," Sabrina said sadly, her eyes glistening with tears. "It would be no different than here."

"It would be a lot different, Mom. There's nothing for you to do here, without Dad. And now you're stuck here at the beach, isolated. You're not going to the gallery. You love the museums in Paris, the galleries, you love walking all over Paris. It would be so great for you. That's what Dad wanted for you. That was what he was trying to tell you that day on the iPad." They both remembered it well, it had been near the end, and Sabrina had paid no attention to the suggestion. She was dreading what they all knew would happen next, and he knew it too. An apartment in Paris meant nothing at that point in time compared to the rest. She would have given everything she had to save his life, and no one could. ALS was a death sentence, a fight they couldn't win.

"I don't want to be in Paris without him," she said firmly,

and Lizzie decided to back off. She could always bring it up at another time.

"Then why don't you take a trip to visit us? Come see me in New York, you can visit Coco in Milan, and Justin in London. We'd love to see you." Sabrina looked thoughtful listening to her daughter. She liked the idea.

"I'll think about it," was all she would commit to. "Maybe in the spring." Lizzie was desperate to get her mother out of the house.

"You need a plan, Mom, so you'll do it. Otherwise you're just going to sit here feeling like shit for the next six months." Or a year . . . or ten . . . but she didn't say that to her mother.

"I'd feel guilty having fun without him."

"Why? It's what he would want, for you to go on living, not bury yourself. You're young, you need to get out and see life and people and the world around you. But first, come and visit us. We'll have some nice time together in New York. And then you can visit the others." Lizzie knew that if she could pull her mother out of the tomb where she had isolated herself, she would start to live again. The house in Malibu was beautiful, but she was burying herself alive, out of survivor guilt and grief. But visiting her children seemed respectable even to her.

Lizzie told the others what she had done after the

conversation, and both Coco and Justin thanked her and agreed with her.

"I think Paris is too big a step for her right now," Lizzie said. "But even getting her to New York would be a victory. It's killing her, just sitting here and crying over him." All three of them knew it was true. After spending almost a week with her over Christmas, they could see how far down a black hole she was. Too far down to dig herself out. She needed help. Lizzie had reached a hand out to her, and she didn't intend to let go. She was going to keep pushing her until she got her mother out. If she were going to her gallery and engaged with that, it would be different. But she wasn't. She had cut herself off from everything and everyone, and had retreated into seclusion. She was drowning in her sorrow, and couldn't find her way out in the dark.

Coco and Justin flew out the next morning, after a warm cozy dinner the night before with food from Mr. Chow. Sabrina got up to see each of them off at five and six o'clock in the morning, just as she always had. She got up at any hour to see them off. Lizzie left that afternoon, and Sabrina held her tight before she left and thanked her for all her help. All three of her children had been wonderful to her while they were there. She was profoundly sad as she watched Lizzie drive her rented car down the driveway while she waved, and the tears flowed liberally once she was alone again. Lizzie had reminded her again before she left to think about visiting her in New York. One step at a time.

Sabrina was so depressed after they left that she didn't eat dinner that night, which wasn't unusual for her. She skipped more meals than she ate now. She went straight to bed, and woke up at two o'clock in the morning, wide awake. She thought of everything Lizzie had said to her, especially about the fact that her getting a place in Paris was Malcolm's last wish. She knew she wasn't ready for that. But she had warmed to the idea of seeing her children in their respective cities. Maybe she could pull that off without falling apart. She could just see her three children and come home, and it might be a fun trip to three different cities that she loved. She didn't have to go to Paris at all.

Sabrina was awake for the rest of the night, her mind racing. She felt as though she could handle it. And the reward for every leg of the trip would be seeing one of her children in each place. She made a cup of tea at seven, and called the airline with the cup in her hand. They had a seat to New York the day after New Year's Day. She booked it online and felt very brave. It was a first. She was not used to fending for herself. Malcolm had always made all their arrangements, and planned all their trips. Sometimes he even surprised her. This time she was surprising herself.

But she knew that Lizzie was right. She had to do something to get herself out of the deep black hole she had been in for six months. It was only going to get worse if she didn't. And Lizzie had struck a chord. Malcolm would not have wanted her to be miserable and lock herself away for the rest of her life.

She booked all the tickets, starting with New York. From there she would visit Coco in Milan, and Justin in London. She would finally meet Arabella, whom he was so taken with. Then she'd fly back to L.A. She didn't want to look at apartments in Paris. Maybe one day, but not now. She booked the hotels at the same time. The Carlyle in New York, the Four Seasons near the Via Montenapoleone in Milan, and Claridge's in London, all her and Malcolm's favorite places, except for Paris. Then she sent Lizzie a text and told her she had booked all the reservations. Lizzie congratulated her for being so brave, and thanked her for coming to see her in New York. She knew the others would be pleased too. They had all been worried about her, especially after seeing her at Christmas. They all wanted to see her get moving again. It was going to be hard for Sabrina without their father, but fate had dealt her a tough hand and she had no choice but to play it. At forty-eight, she couldn't give up on life. Sabrina realized it now too. Moving forward without Malcolm was going to be the hardest thing she'd ever done. But she knew she had to, for her children's sake, and her own.

Sabrina called Hallie to tell her she was leaving on a trip to see her children. She thought that she'd be gone for about three weeks, and she promised to come to the gallery when she got back, and apologized for staying away for so long. Hallie didn't know what had happened or what had changed, but she could tell that Sabrina had turned a corner. She was coming back to life again. It was going to be painful for her without Malcolm, but she was taking her first steps back on the road to life, and Hallie hoped the trip would go well for her.

Hallie booked a car to take Sabrina to the airport, and she left the day after New Year's as planned. Sabrina looked out the window at L.A. below her as the plane took off, saw the myriad of swimming pools like shimmering jewels beneath her as the plane headed for New York, and as hard as it was to be going without him, knew that Malcolm would approve.

Chapter 3

With the time difference, Sabrina got to New York at five P.M., and after collecting her bags, arrived at the Carlyle at seven P.M. after rush hour traffic on the way into the city. They gave her a very pretty suite that she and Malcolm had had before, and she called Lizzie immediately. She had just gotten home from the library and sounded stressed.

"Are you okay?" Sabrina asked her.

"Yes, just annoyed. We started back today, and I had two classes that assigned us papers on the first day back, due on Friday. And a third one where they're giving us an exam next week. They do it all the time to see how prepared we are. I have a feeling they're going to pile the work on right to the last day."

"Do you still want to do dinner tonight? If you have too much work, I understand." Sabrina was tired herself from the trip. She hadn't traveled in months, and it was harder without Malcolm. He always took care of the details, now she had to. Lizzie insisted she could make time for dinner, and she'd work on her papers afterward.

Sabrina took a cab to Lizzie's apartment near Columbia. The building was awful, and the neighborhood too far uptown, but the apartment was decent, and Lizzie had fixed it up nicely. It was a comfortable place to study. She never entertained friends, so she had never done much with it, and her time at Columbia was almost over now. She had five months before graduation, and they were going to wring every drop of work out of her before she finished. She had earned her law degree with blood, sweat, and tears, and could hardly wait for it to end.

Sabrina offered to pick up food on the way uptown and arrived laden with packages from Zabar's. It was fancy deli food, and Lizzie was ravenous. They had dinner in her kitchen, and then Sabrina left her to get started on the first paper she had to do. An hour later, Sabrina was in bed and happy to be there. She woke up at eight o'clock the next morning, walked down Madison Avenue after breakfast, did some shopping at Bergdorf Goodman, and then went back to the hotel, waiting to hear from Lizzie after her classes. Lizzie called at four on the way to the library to do some research for her paper, and didn't call again until after nine, sounding exhausted, and offered to come by the hotel to see her mother. Sabrina felt sorry for her and let her off the hook. They managed to have dinner the following night, and Lizzie had been given another paper to do for another class. Sabrina realized that her presence in New York was more of a burden for Lizzie than a pleasure and decided to leave the next day for Milan. She felt terrible about all the work Lizzie had to do, and her worry about entertaining her mother on top of it. Lizzie sounded relieved when Sabrina said she was leaving early.

Sabrina called the airline to change her flight, went uptown to see Lizzie one last time, and left on a midnight flight to Milan. She slept on the plane. She was traveling in first class, and the Four Seasons had arranged for a car and driver to take her to the hotel when she arrived in Milan. She had texted Coco to say she was coming early, and Coco worked until midnight that night and they had breakfast together the next day. Prada's staff were up to their ears doing fittings and picking models for their show for Fashion Week with the fall/winter collection. Milan was bustling with press and models and editors arriving for the show. Coco was working until midnight every night, and one night till two A.M., and had to be back at work at eight o'clock every morning. She looked exhausted but it was exciting for her to be there, helping to prepare the collection.

It took Sabrina two days to realize that the timing of her visit was terrible for Coco. She spent a day shopping on the Via Montenapoleone, and decided to leave for London earlier than planned. Her children were so busy with their jobs and school that she felt like a burden to them just being there. It was more stressful than enjoyable for her daughters to have her hovering, waiting for a chance to see them, which defeated the purpose of spending some time together. With final papers due and exams before graduation from law school for Lizzie, and the madness of Fashion Week for Coco, these were exceptional circumstances, and real life for both of them. It reminded Sabrina yet again that they were adults with heavy responsibilities and demands on their time. Lizzie couldn't have predicted the new assignments she'd be given, and Coco was an intern who was expected to work incredible hours right before a show. Coco was sorry that she was leaving, but grateful that her mother understood the demands she had to meet for her job.

Sabrina arrived at Claridge's in London and texted Justin. He was struggling with papers and exams too. Her children were hardworking, conscientious, and responsible, and she spent two days shopping in London before Justin had time to see her. He met her at a trendy little restaurant and brought Arabella to meet her. She was a lovely, polite, well-brought-up, intelligent young woman who captured Sabrina's heart immediately. Sabrina was happy to meet her at last, and at dinner it was obvious from the way they held hands and looked at each other that they were deeply in love. Justin was besotted with her, and she had a good job and was working hard. And it wasn't lost on Sabrina that Arabella looked a little bit like her and was tall and blonde. They had a very pleasant time at dinner, and then Justin had to go home and study for an exam the next day. None of them could have predicted how much work their bosses and professors would give them, especially Lizzie and Justin in the final stretch before their graduations in May and June. Sabrina was planning to come back for their graduation ceremonies, but she doubted that either of them would have time to see her until then. And then they'd be off and running in their first jobs. Justin was interviewing now at American firms with London offices, where he could get a visa more easily.

Sabrina marveled at how hard her children were working, and knew that Malcolm would have been proud of them too. The idea of visiting them had been a good one, but the timing didn't work for them, although they did their best to see her whenever they had free time. She felt guilty for interrupting their work, and taking up time they didn't have. She hated to go home early having barely seen them, and at the last minute decided to go to Paris after all. It was such a short trip from London. She flew instead of taking the train. She called the Ritz and they had a suite for her, and suddenly the prospect of sinking into the luxurious comforts of the Ritz was immensely appealing. She booked a flight and that afternoon she checked into the Ritz, after racing by Justin's apartment to give him a quick hug and kiss before she left.

"I'm so sorry, Mom," he apologized. "I didn't think I'd be this slammed." He felt terrible about it.

"It's my fault. I should have guessed." But she was glad she'd come anyway, even for a glimpse of them as they rushed past her like express trains, flying through their busy lives. It was comforting that they were happy, doing what they loved. She knew they loved her, and worried about her, but there was understandably no room for her in their daily lives right now. She was only a burden to them, but it felt good to be out in the world again. She realized now how secluded and disconnected and isolated she had been in the last seven months. This trip made it clear to her that she needed to make her own life. She couldn't depend on them to keep her company or fill the giant void that Malcolm had left when he died. It wasn't their fault, any more than it was hers or Malcolm's. They were adults, living in other cities with overfull lives, appropriate to their age and stage in life.

It was a cold, crisp day in Paris, and she took a walk around the Place Vendôme and to the Tuileries Gardens before ordering room service for a delicious dinner. She'd spent a busy ten days going to all three cities and seeing very little of her children, but it was the best they could do. They were one busier than the next, entirely appropriately, given the final days of their studies and Coco's new internship.

Sabrina was happy to be in Paris and have some time to herself. The suite they'd given her was one she and Malcolm had stayed in, but she didn't mind. It reminded her of the good times she'd had there with him. It shocked her to realize that it was exactly a year since he had experienced the first signs of ALS and their search for a diagnosis had begun. And now he was gone, and her life looked like a long, lonely stretch of road ahead of her. She had no plan for the future, and no desire to organize one. Nothing she had done before would be fun or meaningful to her without Malcolm. She had no idea what one did when one lost the love of one's life. She had their children, but they had just reminded her that they had their own lives. And without Malcolm she had none. She didn't know what the answer was. All she knew was that she wanted to come to Paris. Their last happy days had been here, before the diagnosis. She realized now that she was looking for a way to turn the film back to the happy part, before it became a horror movie. She felt numb now, grateful for her children, and heartbroken over Malcolm. There was no way to hide from the pain, so she had come back to the Ritz to remember their last carefree moments only a year before.

She lay in bed thinking about him that night until she fell asleep. She didn't know it yet, but the healing had begun. She had put one foot back in the world, in Paris at the Ritz. She didn't know how long it would take to bring the other foot forward too. She felt rooted to the spot where grief had led her, and Malcolm had left her. And she had no idea how long it would take her to learn to walk again without him. She couldn't even imagine it yet.

Coco called her from Milan when she woke up. She was on her way to the office, still working on the show. Sabrina had seen how much she loved her job and was happy for her.

"I just wanted to make sure you got to Paris okay. What are you going to do there?" Coco asked her.

"I don't know yet." Sabrina didn't want to say "cry," which

was probably true. She had cried on her walk the day before. But the tears were different now. They were more bitter-sweet than signs that she was drowning. She was treading water now, not sure which way to go.

"Why don't you look at some apartments, or a house?" Coco suggested.

"I don't want to live alone here," Sabrina said quietly. "It made sense with your father. It doesn't now." She said it as simple fact, but Coco knew she wouldn't be happy in Malibu either. Malcolm had left his mark there too. Paris was a clean slate Sabrina could write on, despite her many visits there with Malcolm, because they both loved it. Nothing made sense without him, but Paris was a beautiful city and she was always happy there. She spoke very little French, but enough to get by in restaurants and taxis. After they hung up, she ordered coffee and toast, and looked out the window at the Place Vendôme. It was raining, but Paris was beautiful even in the rain. The light softened it, like a luminous gray pearl.

She called the concierge then, and asked him to book a car and driver for her, and for the name of a reliable realtor. They hung up and he called her five minutes later and gave her two names.

"I think they both speak English. Our clients have used them before. One of them, the second one, specializes in temporary apartments, mostly for Americans. The other one is for people who want to buy homes here."

"Thank you," she said, sitting at the desk, hesitating, and decided to call the one who handled real estate purchases. She was connected to a Mme. Troquet, who sounded older and spoke perfect English with a British accent, as many people in France did. Sabrina told her she wanted to see an apartment in good condition with four or five bedrooms, and a view would be nice. Not a walk-up.

"Any particular neighborhood?"

"The eighth, the sixteenth, the seventh, or the first," Sabrina said firmly. She knew Paris well, and she and Malcolm had liked those areas best. One was on the Left Bank, and three were on the Right.

"We have some listings that might suit you," Mme. Troquet said. "I'll check on them and get back to you." Sabrina thanked her and went to shower. She knew it was a futile exercise and she wouldn't buy anything, but it didn't hurt to look.

Mme. Troquet called as Sabrina was getting out of the shower. "Three of the listings are still available," she said in a cool voice. "One isn't." Sabrina told herself it was just something to do to satisfy her children, and say she had done it. She didn't want an apartment in Paris without Malcolm. She knew that much. They'd looked at apartments there before in the past few years, and never found anything they fell in love with. And they wanted it to be a love match if they bought in Paris.

Sabrina wrote down the address where she was to meet the realtor, dressed, and an hour later got in the car waiting for her downstairs. The driver looked serious and was older, with white hair, was wearing a black suit, and spoke adequate English. He said his name was Jean.

He took her to the address she gave him, on the Left Bank. It was on the rue de Varenne, not far from the Rodin Museum, which she knew well. The realtor was waiting for her and had the keys to all three apartments she wanted Sabrina to see. They were her listings. The first apartment was large, in good condition, and not exciting. It was a little dark, and Sabrina said no quickly. It had no charm. The other two they saw were on the Avenue Montaigne and the Avenue Foch. The one on the Avenue Montaigne was being sold by a Russian, the one on the Avenue Foch by a Saudi family. Both were a little too ornate for Sabrina. The one on the Avenue Montaigne had a perilous-looking marble staircase. It looked glamorous but dangerous to Sabrina. Neither of them appealed to her. She didn't know what she wanted, if anything, but she knew what she didn't. But she could tell her children she had seen three apartments, and didn't like them. There was nothing warm and inviting about them. They didn't feel like home and two were too fancy, although the buildings were handsome and the locations were good. She didn't bother to ask the prices since she didn't want them. They seemed sterile and showy. She didn't think Malcolm would have liked them either. They would have bought something chic and charming, and these weren't either.

Sabrina went for a walk that afternoon, thinking about what she'd seen, and she had an idea. She spoke to the concierge when she got back, and asked about renting a car. She suddenly wanted to see countryside, maybe some châteaux, she wanted to breathe some air. She and Malcolm had taken several driving trips around France, visiting châteaux. She wanted to get out of the city. Maybe to Normandy or Deauville. She asked the concierge to rent a car for her for the next day, something comfortable.

"Do you know where you want to go?"

"Maybe Deauville." It wasn't far, about two hours away. "I want to see the ocean."

"Have you been to Biarritz, madame?" he asked her. "It's a longer drive, but it's quite beautiful and there's a wonderful hotel there. It was the summer palace of Napoleon the Third and Empress Eugénie. They've turned it into a five-star hotel. It's remarkable."

"How long a drive is it?" she asked.

"Seven hours, but it's beautiful, in the Basque country. And the beaches are lovely."

"Thank you." She didn't know where she wanted to go and seven hours seemed long, but the hotel sounded interesting. She just wanted to get in the car and drive and see where she wound up. She had total freedom now, to go wherever she wanted. It was both frightening and exciting at the same time. Her life with Malcolm had been so carefully planned and predictable, which had made her feel secure. Now everything had turned upside down, and in a way it freed her to do anything that came to mind, without a plan.

She slept well that night again, and had room service for dinner. She packed a small bag in the morning, in case she wanted to stay somewhere on the way, and she went to the concierge to pick up the keys to the rented car and sign the papers he had for her.

"Have you decided where you're going, madame?" he asked her, and she smiled.

"I think I'll just see where I wind up," she said. He nodded, and she went out to claim the car and put her bag in the back. A few minutes later she was crossing Paris to the Porte d'Orléans on her way out of the city. She had set the GPS for Biarritz. She didn't have to go all the way, and she could change her mind anytime. It was an unfamiliar sensation, but she was enjoying her freedom.

She turned onto the A10 freeway and followed the signs. The GPS told her where to go, and in a short time she was in the countryside. There were cows and farms and she was enjoying it. She was surprised when she noticed she had been driving for three hours. She had passed a church that she recognized. She and Malcolm had had a picnic there on one of their romantic trips. They had visited the Tours Cathedral on one of their driving trips, and in the course of the day, she drove on past the châteaux de Chambord, Blois, and Chenonceau, all of which she and Malcolm had been to and enjoyed.

She stopped and bought a sandwich and a bottle of water at a gas station, kept driving, and at three that afternoon, saw a sign that said she was fifty kilometers from Biarritz. She was almost there and had been driving for six hours. It took another forty-five minutes to get to Biarritz. She smiled when she saw the Hôtel du Palais. She recognized it immediately. It was an enormous palace on the Atlantic Coast, and she noticed that there were surfers in the water in wetsuits. The beach was wide, the ocean was beautiful, and there were few people on the beach at that time of the year, only the surfers and people with their dogs. It made her want to take her shoes off and walk in the sand. It hadn't been a hard drive and she loved where she had landed. She loved the grandeur of Napoleon and Empress

Eugénie's summer palace. It was a pretty little town of twenty-five thousand people.

The palace had been built in 1855, and Biarritz was twenty miles from the Spanish border in the Pyrénées. The town itself looked somewhat luxurious with fancy shops and many restaurants, and had a slightly old-fashioned, historical feeling to it. She'd seen on the internet that the beach was five miles long, and that there were tall cliffs, several museums, and two very popular casinos. It was a perfect resort town, as Napoleon and Empress Eugénie had decided too. Sabrina couldn't help thinking that she would have loved to see it when Napoleon's court was there nearly two hundred years before, with all the carriages pulling up to it, with grand people arriving for a ball at night. Now it was just a pretty beach town with a fabulous hotel. She decided that it was worth staying there for a night, just to see it. She wondered what the suites were like. Biarritz had been in and out of fashion for the past two hundred years, and was somewhere in between now. Not nearly as elegant or in fashion as the south of France, the Côte d'Azur, but it had an undeniable grandeur with the Hôtel du Palais dominating the scene.

Sabrina googled it from her phone and smiled as she read about it. She knew Malcolm would have loved it, and she wished they had discovered it together. But now the memory of it would belong only to her.

Google informed her that Biarritz had six beaches and many parks. There was also an Imperial Chapel built for Empress Eugénie, and Sabrina was eager to see if it had beautiful frescoes and murals, which were her passion.

Sabrina drove to the hotel, asked at the front desk if there was a suite available, and they said there was, and she checked in. She went to get her bag from her car, sent the car to the garage, and went to claim her room. She couldn't wait to see it. When the bellboy who accompanied her opened the door for her, the sweeping view of the ocean took her breath away. The sun was setting by then, and there was a red glow in the sky. It was a magical setting, which combined natural beauty and man-made grandeur on a huge scale. The suite they had given her was elegant and old-fashioned. She felt a million miles from anything familiar, which was exactly what she had wanted. Everything she knew or loved had been broken and disappeared, and she had wanted to see something new and different. Biarritz fit that description. Nothing about it was familiar.

She stood staring at the ocean from her windows, and saw the surfers coming in for the night. They looked like seals in their black wetsuits, carrying their boards.

She decided not to order room service that night, and

decided to explore. She didn't want a meal in the hotel's fancy dining room. She preferred to walk and find a little bistro, which she did, and had a delicious bowl of bouilla-baisse made from local fish. She sat at a small table and no one bothered her. She normally didn't like eating alone in restaurants, and never did, but the town felt safe, and the waiters at the restaurant were nice and respectful. The whole town had a good feeling.

She walked past the casinos after dinner, but had no desire to enter. Neither she nor Malcolm were gamblers, and she suspected that the crowd there would be flashy. She was enjoying strolling around the town, and she stopped when she saw a realtor's office tucked between two buildings, a restaurant and a small hotel, and she carefully looked at the photographs in the window. There were two or three very large châteaux for sale that had no appeal for her. There were many like them for sale in France, cold and drafty, cumbersome and expensive to run, and usually in need of extensive repairs. There were photographs of several villas too. They were pretty and on a more human scale but nothing out of the ordinary, just summer homes for bankers or dentists or accountants looking for houses in the area.

But the photograph that caught her eye was of a house that looked like a château in a fairy tale. It had turrets and balconies, a graceful roof, and beautiful gardens around it. It was smaller than the other châteaux, but very distinctive-looking. It made Sabrina smile when she saw it. It was just outside a town called Arcangues, five miles from Biarritz. There was another house listed there too, more of a cottage, painted white with bright blue shutters. The little château looked unusual, elegant, and a little eccentric. Whimsical was the word it evoked as she looked at the photograph. It was bigger than she'd want, but it appealed to her. It made her want to check out the little town five miles away. The château she liked was the Château de Bonport, and in English below it someone had written the translation, Château of Safe Harbor. She wondered if it was still for sale, and for how much. The photograph looked old. She put the realtor's number in her phone and walked away. It was just a crazy idea, and she forgot about it as she walked back to the hotel. She'd had a nice evening in the town. Biarritz had a good feeling, and was a wonderful contrast to Paris. It made her feel very adventuresome, having come alone.

She remembered Arcangues again and the château when she got back to the hotel and looked it up on her laptop. Arcangues was a town built in the twelfth century, so seven hundred years older than Biarritz, less than five miles away, with three thousand inhabitants. It was described as pretty and peaceful, built around the local church. It had been rebuilt in modern times using original materials from the time it had been built. All of the homes and cottages had blue shutters of a distinctive blue referred to as Arcangues Blue. It was a bright teal with a hint of turquoise to it, unusual and beautiful. There was an inn, a school, and a castle nearby. The church had been built in the sixteenth century, and there was a lovely cemetery where all the headstones were round. Everything about the town looked and sounded quaint and charming, and she decided to go and see it the next day. It looked as though it would definitely be worth the trip. It intrigued her that the bright distinctive blue of the shutters and timbers had been granted as a "right and privilege" to the Marquis of Arcangues in the twentieth century to be used exclusively in Arcangues. She wanted to see it.

Sabrina opened the windows before she fell asleep. She could smell the sea air and hear the ocean outside her windows. She could imagine what it must have been like when Napoleon's court was in residence there in the summer. It would have been a fascinating time to be alive. It was the first time she had ever slept in a palace, and for the first time in seven months, she slept like a child.

Chapter 4

S abrina went back to the realtor's office the next day
and inquired about the photograph in the window. An
older man sitting at a desk rolled his eyes when she asked
about it. He spoke English and was used to foreign tourists.
He told her the château had been on and off the market
several times in the last few years, and he didn't know its
current status. The last he'd heard the owners were living
there during the pandemic, but that was two years ago and
he didn't know if they still were. The château in the photograph was the Château de Bonport.

"It's newer than some of the others we have listed, early
eighteenth-century, and it's smaller than several others, if
you're looking for something grander. We have two very
large ones too. They're not expensive but they need a great

deal of work. The Château de Bonport is in good condition. All it needs is a bit of paint and minor repairs. Maybe they've done that by now. It's between Arcangues and Biarritz. It's lovely in the summer, very pretty gardens if you're looking for a summer home." She had no idea what she was looking for, nothing really. This was not the Paris apartment Malcolm had promised her, but it looked charming and beautiful in the pictures. "Would you like to see it?" he offered. "I can call and find out if it's still listed, or currently occupied by the owners or renters. Things change and people forget to tell us, particularly after all the upheavals of the pandemic."

She thought it might be fun to see, and she had nothing else to do. He called the number he had, and someone told him it was not officially on the market at the moment, but it might be a possibility. They were open to offers. The realtor volunteered to drive Sabrina to see it. The owners were apparently in Paris, but the caretaker was authorized to show it, and the realtor said he could discuss the price with the owners later, if she was interested. The caretaker didn't know if they would sell or rent it.

The realtor drove Sabrina there himself, so she left her car at his office. The sun came out while they were on the way from Biarritz to Arcangues. They passed a monastery with nuns and children outside playing soccer, and Sabrina smiled as she watched them, as one of the children tripped one of the nuns, who was laughing.

"What's that?" Sabrina asked the realtor about the building where the children and nuns were.

"It's a convent. It's been an unofficial orphanage since the pandemic. There are church services there on Sunday, and many other churches in the area, if you're Catholic. The nuns have quite a nice choir with the children, if you like that sort of thing. The nuns take in as many children as they can. Some of them lost their entire families, or they're left with one parent who can't care for them." It sounded sad to Sabrina, and they drove past it quickly toward the Château de Bonport.

Three miles outside Biarritz, just before Arcangues, they went down a long driveway with orchards on either side. There was fruit on the ground, and the orchards didn't look well tended. Sabrina wondered if the house had gone to rack and ruin since the photographs. It was possible. It had been a hard time in France, and everywhere else recently, and maybe the owners were selling because they were out of money.

They followed a bend in the road, and the house came into view. It was just as lovely as the photograph, and the gardens were only slightly less well tended, but still very handsome. There were big trees all around the property, and Sabrina could see a long lawn behind the house with more gardens, surrounded by tall trees.

There were several smaller houses on the property, one larger than the others, not too near the main building. The realtor explained that this was the dower house, where the current owner's widowed mother usually stayed once her son inherited the château after his father's death, which automatically relegated his mother to the smaller home. Sabrina was familiar with dower houses from trips to England, where they had the same tradition.

The château itself was beautiful, and larger in person than it appeared in the photograph, but it wasn't enormous or daunting. It still had the same fairy-tale quality which had attracted her attention and appealed to her. It was very much of the period and well-preserved despite the sea air. And it looked just as magical and whimsical as it had in the photograph she had seen the night before in the window.

An old man came toward them when they stopped the car and identified himself to the realtor as the caretaker. His name was Maxime. He was carrying a huge antique ring of keys, and led the way up the steps to the front door, which had an enormous brass knocker that Sabrina noticed needed polishing. And when the door opened, she saw ancestral portraits, a long hall, some hunting trophies, and tapestries, some in better shape than others. The realtor explained, "The French call this in 'its own juice.' Everything is original, just the way they inherited it for generations." The furniture was all antique, the rooms were sunny, and the curtains elegant and a little frayed. Everything looked well used, a little shabby, but the overall feeling was cozy and inviting. It looked as though one could be at home there, and obviously people were. There was a skateboard in the front hall, some tennis rackets, and a set of golf clubs. The realtor said there was a golf course which encircled the town, if she played golf. It looked like someone's home, not a relic of the ancient past or a museum. Sabrina felt at ease and welcome as soon as she walked in, almost as though the small, pretty château put its arms around her and embraced her. There was evidence that the residents had been using the fireplaces, but the caretaker assured them that there was modern heating and plumbing throughout the house, the pipes were good and the roof was sound, and there were new appliances in the kitchen. So it had the charm of an old château but the convenience of a modern home, one that looked well lived in and a little beaten up. But something about it touched Sabrina, far more than the fancy apartments she'd been shown in Paris that had no soul. They were devoid of life and traces of the people who lived there. The château looked homey and loved.

They walked through the house to the huge lawn behind it, and Sabrina wandered to the edge of the gardens and took a deep breath of the fresh air. The sea was only a few miles away and you could smell it. She could imagine her own children lounging in the chairs on the patio behind the main house, or running on the lawn, chasing each other in some game. They went back inside and upstairs. There were half a dozen very handsome bedrooms, most of which were unoccupied, and a dozen smaller rooms on the floor above, for servants in the past, many of them used as store-rooms now for sports equipment, luggage, a giant telescope, and antique furniture no longer used but original to the house.

It took an hour to take the full tour, and Sabrina felt a little intrusive going from room to room. The owners clearly had children, she wasn't sure how many, and there was a very pretty young girl's room at the opposite end from the master suite. There was also a second master suite near it, with a closet full of women's clothes. There were only men's clothes in the main master suite at the opposite end, with a man's riding boots, tennis shoes, tweed jackets, some blazers, a leather bomber jacket that looked vintage, and stacks of books everywhere.

They had seen it all by the time they left. The realtor had inquired again if it was still for sale.

"The missus told me to show it if anyone ever called. The master doesn't want to sell it, it's his family's home. They've been living here since the pandemic, but they go to Paris too. She's there most of the time. She's a doctor. He stays here whenever he can." The master suite looked well occupied, with many stacks of books. There were still two horses in the stable, and the caretaker said he took care of them. Even though it was a château, it was clearly a family home. Sabrina had the sudden feeling that Malcolm would have loved it, and would have wanted to clean it all up and bring it back to its full glory. She didn't mind it looking a little worn. It felt more inviting to her that way, and less lonely than if everything had been perfect.

They thanked Maxime for his time, and went back to the realtor's office for her car.

"It needs a little tidying up, and some paint here and there. Many of the châteaux we see aren't in as good shape as this one, and haven't been inhabited in years, and would take a lot of work to restore," the realtor commented.

"I'll give it some thought," she promised when she left.

"I'll speak to them about a price," he said, but it didn't make sense to her. It was a crazy idea, and just because it had charm wasn't a reason to buy it. She didn't need it and it was a long way from home. She had no real use for a château in Biarritz, seven hours from Paris, no matter how charming it was. It might be fun to rent for a summer, but her children loved the polished glamour and sophistication of the south of France, not a country château.

There was a small swimming pool, considerably smaller than the one she had in Malibu. The property was very French and looked original, from the furniture to the scale and design of the château.

Sabrina was quiet all the way back to the realtor's office. She was thinking of the rooms she'd seen at the château. It had been so warm and welcoming. But the whole idea seemed absurd. What would she do with a château in the Pays Basque area in France, near the Pyrénées?

"I'll let you know what I hear from the owners," the realtor said, lumbering back to his desk, and Sabrina thanked him and drove away in her rented car. She didn't head back to Biarritz but drove the short distance back toward Arcangues, to get a feel for the picturesque quality of the area, and visit the town. She drove past the gates of the Château de Bonport. They were still open, but all she could see were the trees lining the driveway, far from the château. She passed the monastery. The soccer game was over, and the nuns and children had gone inside, so she didn't see them, but she could hear choir practice. They sounded like angels, the children's voices blending with the nuns'.

Within a mile, she saw the church at the center of the town come into view, the sixteenth-century Church of Saint John the Baptist, and the terraced cemetery with round flat headstones like disks.

She got out and walked around, and the little village had a wonderful feel to it. In the distance were the Pyrénées. She saw the town hall, the school, and the inn, all with their brilliant blue shutters, distinctive to the village, and different from any neighboring town. There was a castle in Arcangues too. Although small, the village seemed very complete. She got back in her car after she'd seen most of it, and drove back to the more worldly splendor of Biarritz.

Arcangues was a relic of the past, and Biarritz had been modernized and brought into the current century. The two were worlds apart in style and feeling. And bridging the two was the Château de Bonport, historic but comfortable and livable. She would have liked to curl up with a good book near the fire on a cold winter night. There was something about the Château de Bonport that had spoken to her, as though it was reaching out to her. She had always believed that houses had a soul, and knew all the secrets of the family who lived there. She thought Malcolm would have loved it, or would he have thought it utterly crazy? Part of her thought that too. This was completely different from anything she had envisioned or thought she'd want.

She drove past the château gates again, and the monastery, on her way back to the Hôtel du Palais in Biarritz. It felt familiar when she saw it. She went to her room and packed her bag, and checked out at the front desk.

"Did you enjoy your stay, madame?" the assistant manager asked her.

"Very much. It's a wonderful place." He smiled and took the key from her, and she walked out carrying her bag and put it in her car.

She had a long drive ahead of her, back to Paris, but she didn't mind. Driving soothed her, and watching the Basque countryside slip by. She had a lot to think about. She had a house in Malibu, and a gallery nearby in L.A. Everything in her life had made sense when Malcolm was there, and made no sense now without him. Her gallery had been so much fun and brought her so much joy, as long as he was around to cheer her on. And without him nothing seemed like fun anymore. She didn't want to close her gallery. She had lost touch with all her friends in the past year, between Malcolm's sudden illness and his death. She didn't have the energy to see them yet, or the strength or desire to endure their pity. They might have lent her support in the last year, but she didn't let them. She had needed to be alone to process the shock of what had happened to Malcolm so quickly. She still couldn't believe it. And with most of their friends their common bond was their children, and all of hers were gone now, moved on to more interesting lives and greener pastures. She felt as though she had nothing to offer anyone now. She was too bruised in the deepest parts of her soul to see anyone. She and Malcolm had had the best marriage of anyone they knew, and now he was gone. She was sad, but she was angry too, not at Malcolm, but at life. They had been cheated of the long years they planned to be together. She had been robbed of their future.

She was thinking about all of it as she drove back to Paris. And as they had on the way down, the seven hours sped by. She felt like she was coming home, when Paris came into view, all lit up at night, with the Eiffel Tower sparkling to greet her. It was a magnificent city. Malibu was a sleepy town by the sea where she could hide, and she had the gallery to amuse her in L.A. Paris was an exciting city and felt alive.

It was late when she got back to the Ritz. She ordered some soup from room service and went to bed afterward. She lay awake for a long time that night thinking about Biarritz, the Château de Bonport, and the tiny medieval village of Arcangues near it with its bright blue shutters.

But Malibu was home, and she knew she had to go back there. Buying a château in France was pure fantasy, she reminded herself. She had almost lost her mind for a minute. She had felt so at home in the little gem of a château. But it was someone else's dream and someone else's home. Malcolm had wanted her to buy an apartment in Paris, not a fairy-tale castle in Arcangues. She had her answer and made her decision. She was going home.

Chapter 5

The apartment on the rue de Sèvres was in a fashionable, trendy location in the 7th arrondissement on the Left Bank, but the building had been allowed to deteriorate, and had a seedy, shabby look. The hallways were dingy and dark and there was no elevator, and the apartment was small, with tiny rooms and an oppressive feeling. The building was narrow, squeezed between two much nicer small apartment buildings in better condition. The woman who had lived there had died at ninety-two. It had been her home for sixty years and she hadn't painted, fixed, or renovated anything since she moved in. It was filthy when her family emptied it and returned it to the building owners, and it was desperately in need of paint. The owners didn't bother, and assumed that a new tenant could clean the

place up and paint it at their own expense. Only the refriger-
ator had been recently replaced, and was the cheapest one
available and already not working well.

It was a brutal change from the spacious duplex Brigitte
and Xavier de Bonport had sold on the Champ de Mars in
an impeccable building, at a prestigious address. They got
less than they should have for it, but it was at the height
of the pandemic and they needed the money. They'd sold
most of their furniture, put the rest in storage, and furnished
the apartment with the bare minimum, leaving their
remaining silver and china in boxes stacked nearly to the
ceiling. It was a temporary move and they didn't plan to
stay there for long. Moving during the worst of the
pandemic, during the lockdown, was complicated and
Brigitte and Xavier had to move quickly when they sold
their apartment. The couch they had moved with them had
sagging springs and battered upholstery, the two big club
chairs were handsome but mismatched. It was depressing
being there, but they were living at their second home in
the Pays Basque at the time. They considered the apartment
more of a storage unit and a place to sleep when they were
in Paris, and they were going to look for a small but decent
apartment after the pandemic. It was a rapid and easy
solution at the time, and they rented month to month. They
had been there for more than two years now, much longer

than expected. They preferred having the money from their apartment sale in the bank than spending it on an expensive apartment to replace the one they'd sold. The rental had two small bedrooms, one for them and one for their daughter, Victoire, who was working in Africa at a refugee center as a nurse practitioner. She had no plans to move back to Paris, but they had a room for her when she came home. And Brigitte de Bonport hardly ever stayed there. She was an emergency doctor for Public Health, and ever since the pandemic began, she had worked long shifts and stayed at the hospital, which was easier than sleeping at home in the ongoing crisis. Xavier was rarely in Paris once they'd sold the apartment, since he was no longer working. He had no reason to be there, except when he came for interviews, most of which happened remotely by video now anyway, and not in person.

The apartment had become the symbol of the deterioration of their marriage, which had started under poor circumstances and had been on shaky ground for thirty years. The apartment was no more unpleasant than the state of their union, which had worsened dramatically during the pandemic. They had no plan to do anything about it, except to hang on, grit their teeth, and punish each other, which was what they had been doing more subtly for years. Brigitte had turned into a bitter woman who loved her career and blamed her husband for their currently impoverished status, which was becoming increasingly acute. Her career as a doctor was the only thing that gave her pleasure and satisfaction, but working for Public Health paid her a pittance. She was from a dedicated medical family. Her grandfather had been a greatly respected pulmonary specialist and a famous professor at the Faculté de Médecine. Her father was a respected oncologist and researcher, her mother had been a nurse, and her brother was an extremely successful cardiac surgeon. He was the only member of the family who had made money from his medical talents, as he was a clever businessman as well, and had made excellent investments. Brigitte respected him deeply, and envied the choices he had made. He and Xavier did not get along. Xavier thought him arrogant and pompous, which Brigitte conceded was true, but he had the success to justify it and back it up. Xavier had next to nothing at the moment, except his half of what they'd gotten for the apartment, and that money was going fast, since they were living on it.

Three years before, his situation had been entirely different, which was why Brigitte had stayed married to him. Being married to a very successful man, with the comforts and status that went with it, she had felt compensated for being trapped in a marriage that never should have happened in the first place, but that offered her benefits she wouldn't have had otherwise. Her lofty academic, intellectual medical family had never had money, except for her brother Guillaume, who had a Midas touch with his investments.

Once Xavier became successful after they married, he had been able to offer her a lifestyle she would never have had otherwise, and she enjoyed it more than she expected. They both worked hard and rarely saw each other, so their ill-suited relationship had been tolerable. But Xavier gave up his job and lost his money in the pandemic, and without the trappings he was previously able to offer her, it was a living hell for them both. She never ceased to remind him of the mistakes he had made and what he'd lost, along with her respect. Her brother Guillaume had said right from the beginning of his downfall, and before, that Xavier was insane for the risk he had taken, and he had warned him it would fail. Xavier hadn't listened, because he couldn't stand Guillaume, and the worst had happened. He lost everything. They'd been living in hell ever since. Brigitte had nothing but contempt for him.

Until four years before, Xavier had the golden job everyone in Paris wanted, and even Brigitte had admired his success. It was the only thing she liked about him. He was the CEO of the biggest, most successful ad agency in

Paris, with all the perks that went with it. They had the most important clients in the business, and for years, Xavier had an astronomical salary, and annual bonuses that were bigger than most people's income. He owned no part of the business, but was the highest paid, most respected high-end chief executive employee in France. Everyone respected him, and he could do no wrong. He was approached by two friends, also advertising executives, with a brilliant idea for a start-up in the global travel business, linking all aspects of travel, planes, trains, hotels, with heavy emphasis on the United States and Asia and a fortune to be made, which they thought was a hundred percent risk-free and a sure success. They approached Xavier to consult for them, to show them through the shoals of launching a start-up, and his advice had been sound. He invested in the business, and within a year, they had started to make an impressive amount of money, planned to go public, thought they would make billions, and were well on the road to an amazing success. Xavier decided it no longer made sense to keep a highly paid job. He didn't need the money, and the time he spent running the ad agency cannibalized time he could use working on the start-up, which was much more fun than his staid, predictable job as CEO. He'd done that for years. A year after they launched, Xavier made a bold decision to quit his job. He was riding two horses with one ass, as he put it, and didn't want to anymore. He was working night and day, and wanted to work exclusively on his new business. It was a liberation for Xavier when he quit his job. He'd been a slave to his employers for long enough. He tendered his resignation, and took off for bigger skies, a decision which at first seemed flawless. The start-up had tremendous potential, and took off like a rocket. He put all the money he had into the business. Six months later, the world came to a dead stop and the bottom fell out of his investment. Within months, the billions they would make evaporated, and Xavier lost every penny he'd invested, his entire savings. Every country was locked down. No one could travel. He had taken a huge risk on what he felt was sure success. No one could have predicted the pandemic and the lethal blow it dealt their business. The start-up closed less than two years after the launch that was so promising. And with the pandemic, jobs like the one he had given up as CEO somewhat cavalierly were no longer available. He had burned his bridges and hadn't been able to find another job as CEO then or since. The start-up was an ignominious defeat, and two years after the pandemic, at fifty-six, he hadn't been able to secure another comparable position, in fact, he found none at all. The pandemic had all but killed the economy, and he hadn't hedged his bets. He was essentially destitute. He and Brigitte sold their apartment to have money to live on. The money was running out, and Brigitte was not amused by the sacrifices they had to make. Their miserable apartment was an affront. Xavier had been out of work for three and a half years, and doors weren't opening to him. All he had left was the château that had been in his family for three hundred years and he refused to sell, determined to pass it on to Victoire, as the only inheritance she could look forward to now. He felt it his honor-bound duty to preserve it for her. Brigitte wanted him to sell it. It had been a three-year bitter battle, which Xavier refused to lose to her.

Brigitte, at fifty-eight, was two years older than he was. They had married when he was twenty-six and she was twenty-eight, at the beginning of her medical career. They dated briefly after meeting at a Christmas party, had a blazing hot affair that was entirely sexual, with little else between them, and he had done the honorable thing and married her when she got pregnant and refused to get an abortion. It had never been a love match, but his rocketlike rise to stardom in his field had compensated for it. She had loved the money he made and the lifestyle it gave them. They had respect and prestige. Xavier's parents were impoverished aristocrats, land rich and cash poor. His father was the president of a small bank, and Xavier's success in business was legendary. Xavier and Brigitte never got along but the money he made gave Brigitte a life she'd never had before and made it worth it to her to stay with him. And then he risked and lost it all. She hated him for it.

Their marriage had been a thirty-year battle, and a final descent into hell when he gave up his job and lost his money on the failed start-up. More than three years later, there was nothing left but the bitter taste of ash for both of them. He stayed at the château as much as possible, while she worked in Paris, avoiding him. He was less and less visible in a job market that had all but forgotten him, and he had no way out of the pit he had dug for himself. Divorce was impossible because she would get half of the château and he would be forced to sell it, leaving nothing to give his daughter one day, and being the first member of his family in three centuries to lose the family château and fail to defend their honor. So they were stuck in a dance of mutual hatred and despair, bitterness and anger, and Brigitte never missed an opportunity to remind him of what a failure he was. He had been at low ebb for three years, and saw no way out, less and less every day. Men had lost their lives willingly in similar situations. He had dreams of another start-up, but no money to pursue them. The ugly dumping ground of an apartment was a symbol of the state of their marriage and relationship. Their life in boxes, any semblance of respect gone. He had put a coat of paint on the dirty walls when they moved in, which was all they had ever done for their marriage, whitewashed it as an inadequate solution to solve a situation that was irreparable.

They had barely known each other when they married after dating for three months. Their daughter Victoire was the only bright spot in a marriage that should never have happened. She was a lovely young woman who had grown up like a flower in the scorched earth and debris of her parents' marriage and loved her job as a nurse practitioner in Africa. During the pandemic, he hadn't seen her for two years, and since then she had found a job and life that fulfilled her and where she felt useful, in Zimbabwe. She hadn't seen her parents in a year. Xavier adored her, and her mother did as well. She was where they poured the only love they had in them. They were good parents and terrible partners, and she had dodged the missiles they hurled at each other for all of her life. She was twenty-nine years old, happy in Zimbabwe, and satisfied to live on what she made. She had few needs, and whether her father had a big job or none at all made no difference to her. She didn't have her mother's lust for money. She knew the good man her father was, the kind person and good parent, and would have forgiven him if he had lost the château. She hated to see him so unhappy and punished so cruelly by her mother. He felt honor-bound to save the château for her, whatever it took to do so, and he put up with Brigitte's bitter barbs whenever he saw her, which was as little as possible. They had given up the pretense of friendship or respect. They lived in separate enemy camps, he in the beauty of the Côte Basque, at the château, and Brigitte's entire life centered around the hospital where she practiced. She had been a hero of the pandemic, and was a talented doctor, her only compassion for her patients. She wasted none on Xavier, and thought him undeserving. The loss of his job she considered a final act of idiocy on his part that had cost her too much to forgive. She had loved the lifestyle he had given her and lost. She had loved their magnificent apartment, loved to travel, and enjoyed the envy of her friends.

The realtor called when Xavier was in Paris for a rare visit. He had heard of a job that might be opening up in his old field, at a new ad agency being formed, and had come to Paris for an important business lunch. He hadn't warned Brigitte he was coming and hoped to avoid her. He had gone to the apartment after lunch to pick up some papers he had in files there, and Brigitte was startled to see him when she walked in, took off her coat, tossing it with her white doctor's coat on one of their two chairs, and overheard his conversation with the real estate agent in Biarritz. His words didn't surprise her, but enraged her again as she poured herself a glass of white wine she'd left in the fridge a few days before. She hadn't seen her husband in a month, and neither smiled when they saw each other, as he continued the conversation and ignored her. She didn't offer him any wine.

"It's not for sale," Xavier said firmly, and sparks flew from Brigitte's eyes. She could guess the subject. Time hadn't been kind to her. She worked hard and had worn herself to the bone working for days without a break during the pandemic. She had never invested herself in her looks, and she looked older than her fifty-eight years. She was more interested in her medical career than in beauty, and had never been interested in fashion. She was wearing an ill-fitting gray skirt, heavy boots, and a black sweater that was too big for her. She kept her hair short in no particular style, which looked almost military. Whatever softness or femininity had once been there had vanished years before. She looked as ill-loved and untended as she was, like a garden that hadn't been watered in years. She wore her nails trimmed very short for medical reasons, and didn't bother with manicures. She'd been fighting a war against Covid for years, since it began, and had performed nobly in the crisis, to the great respect of her peers, and even Xavier on that single front. She was an outstanding physician, and a terrible wife.

Xavier was still a handsome man, with dark aristocratic looks, dark brown hair, warm brown eyes, finely chiseled features, and a cleft chin that was decidedly attractive and enhanced his looks, but she no longer cared. He was tall, thin, and athletic-looking. He had been a hard worker when he had a job and stayed fit by doing all the heavy work and repairs at the château. He had nothing else to do now, and it helped buoy his spirits to do something constructive. His morale had suffered severely from three years of hard blows, many of them delivered by his wife, which she thought justified. They had as little left in their emotional reserves as he did in his bank account. And they were still hanging on.

"I might be willing to rent, on condition that I retain use of the dower house on the property," Xavier continued the conversation on the phone. There was a pause then as he frowned, and seemed to be considering something. "I've never thought of a price for a rental," he admitted. "What would you consider the top of the market?" Then another pause. "Fine. Add another twenty percent to that, and I'll rent it. As is. No additions, no repairs, no improvement projects to suit her. Can she afford it?" He knew the woman would be crazy to rent the château at that price, but the realtor said she looked like a rich American. He just hoped she wasn't crazy and wouldn't be a nuisance. "Six months, or a year. No longer. Children?" He looked satisfied by a negative answer. "Full financial references, I don't want a squatter I can't get out. I want to get a look at her. I'll be there tomorrow," he said decisively, and sounded like the businessman he had been and no longer was, much to his chagrin. He had lived with deep humiliation ever since the global travel business failed, and not being able to find another job as CEO in any field. He was afraid he'd been out of work for too long. He felt stale.

"Who was that?" Brigitte asked when he ended the call, as she added more wine to her glass, and again offered him none.

"The realtor in Biarritz." She thought so. "An American woman looked at the château today. He thought she might rent it. He's not sure."

"And you won't sell it." Her jaw tightened.

"He wanted to know our status about selling," Xavier said honestly.

"That's easy. We're broke," she said nastily. He was used to it. She'd never been gentle, and less so now. She was cold and angry, with an anger older than time.

"Thank you for reminding me," he said, tense. "And we're not broke. We have the money from the apartment. We moved into this rat's nest so we could preserve that money. We're lucky Victoire is in Africa and not living with us, fortunately for her."

"And how long do you think the apartment money will last? You keep spending it on maintaining your money pit in Arcangues."

"It will hold us for a while, until I go back to work," he said, trying to retain some semblance of dignity, and pretense of hope.

"And how long has it been? Three years?" she said, slicing through him like a scalpel. He was used to it, but it still hurt anyway.

"It'll last as long as it has to," he said grimly.

"You're not going to find a job, sitting at the château, feeling sorry for yourself." Xavier wasn't staying with her to preserve a marriage, but a house. Their simmering dislike of each other for twenty-seven years had erupted into rage in the last three years, once he gave up his job for the start-up and lost his money. It had turned Brigitte's disrespect and dislike to hatred during the pandemic. The pandemic had changed everything for them. It had made a hero of her as a doctor, and a fool of him in business and in her eyes. She had been tormenting him ever since. And they couldn't afford a divorce, or he would lose the château. It was the only valuable asset he had left. "How much is she willing to pay to rent it?" Brigitte asked him.

"I have no idea. I'll know more tomorrow. If we get a decent rental price, we can live on that for a while, and preserve the money we have left from the apartment sale." Their life was a constant juggling act now. It was exactly the opposite of their life before his start-up failed. While he was CEO of the ad agency, he had a huge salary, bonuses, commissions, investments. They had a beautiful apartment and a golden life. He had gambled it all and lost, and Brigitte would never forgive him for it. The only thing she ever liked about him was the prestige she got from being married to him, and the material benefits, and now all of that was gone.

"If you get a decent rental price from this woman, I'll give you another six months to find a job. And if you don't, I'm done. I want a divorce and you'll have to sell the château and give me half of it. That's it, Xavier. Six months." He listened to her and didn't comment, and started putting some clothes and papers in a small suitcase. She looked surprised. He had just arrived that day. "Where are you going?"

"To Arcangues. I want to get a look at the woman tomorrow and make sure she's sane." He closed the bag, put on his coat, and walked to the front door. He looked at Brigitte and didn't respond to the ultimatum she had just given him, but he had heard her loud and clear. She watched him leave and didn't say goodbye, and neither did he. He closed the door behind him, and she poured herself another glass of wine. He had a seven-hour drive ahead of him that night, for a worthy cause, to buy time, and save his château.

The realtor called Sabrina in her suite at the Ritz. She'd spent the day at the Louvre, and went to Chanel afterward to shop for her daughters. She found nothing for herself and didn't care. She had no one to dress for now.

He told her Xavier's terms. He named a hefty price for the rental of the château, on condition that she allow him to live in the dower house. He would be in Paris part of the time. And for now at least, the château was not for sale. Sabrina was quiet as she thought about it. The monthly rent sounded reasonable to her. She wondered what her children would think, and if they'd like the château in Arcangues, instead of the south of France, for their annual vacation. The château was less glamorous. But it felt like a healing place for her, and she could afford it easily. She squeezed her eyes shut, and wondered what Malcolm would have advised her. She could always buy an apartment in Paris later, and the Château de Bonport was the only place she had liked. It was an hour's flight from Paris, and she could go to the city anytime and stay at the Ritz.

"I'll take it," she blurted out. It felt like a big decision, but there wasn't any risk involved for her. If she hated it, she could go to Paris or back to Malibu. She had nothing to lose. It seemed a little crazy, but her whole life felt crazy now. "I want to see it one more time. I'll fly down tomorrow, and if I like it, I'll rent it for a year." She could fly to France from L.A., whenever she wanted to. She was free to do as she wished, and she could afford to.

"I'll pass the message on to the owner," he said solemnly. "He'll be here tomorrow, and he'd like to meet you."

"That's fine," she agreed, and they both hung up. She called the concierge then to arrange an early morning flight to Biarritz.

Xavier drove to Arcangues that night, to get a look at the crazy American woman the next day. He wanted to clean the place up a bit before she saw it again, maybe put some flowers around the house, but mostly to get a look at her. If she rented the château, it gave him another six months to find a job, and money to live on. It would give him a reprieve, after three years of bad luck. And there was still enough money left from the sale of their handsome apartment to support them for some time. Rent for the château would help him stretch that for a while.

Things weren't quite as dire as Brigitte made them out, although they were pretty bad. He hadn't been able to find a job in three years, and at fifty-six, he was beginning to doubt that he ever would. His days as CEO of a large, important company seemed to have come to an end. They had had a sizable amount of money from the sale of the apartment, and about half of it was left. He wasn't thrilled at the idea of splitting what remained with Brigitte, but that wasn't the worst of it. She wanted him to sell the château and split that with her, cheating their only child of the only valuable asset they had to give her, and robbing her of her ancestral history. Xavier would not let that happen, even if it meant staying married to a woman who hated him to protect that asset for his daughter.

He had missed their elegant apartment at first, but had learned to live without it. The miserable apartment they had rented on the rue de Sèvres to take its place was a travesty. And without the apartment, he had lost his Parisian life. But the Château de Bonport was not just a piece of real estate to him. It was his ancestral heritage and his daughter's. It was in his blood, and was a sacred responsibility he'd been given to protect for future generations, Victoire's children and grandchildren. It meant nothing to Brigitte, who didn't have the same sense of history or family. The only thing she understood and respected was medicine. She had been a vital force saving lives during the pandemic and he readily agreed that human lives were more important than houses, even historical ones. There was nothing in Brigitte's life or family that meant as much to her. She liked the status expensive belongings gave her, but she didn't care about the ancestral bond that he had been taught to love and respect. It was just a house to her, and she'd rather have the money. She had no conscience about forcing him to sell it, a sure thing in a divorce, which he was trying to avoid at all cost. He felt he owed it to his ancestors, his daughter, and the children she would have one day to preserve it. It was the only thing he had that mattered. Brigitte had tried to convince their daughter how ridiculous and meaningless it was, just a pile of old stones in an old town in the Pyrénées, and money in the bank would be better and less troublesome.

But Victoire was more traditional than that. She was her father's daughter and she had deep affection for the noble home she would inherit one day, and felt the same responsibility for it that Xavier did. Her mother hadn't found an ally in her. Brigitte knew she would never make a fortune practicing medicine, so she wanted to squeeze Xavier for whatever she would get, and the château was all he had left of any value, after his fiasco with the start-up. She resented every penny he had lost. It was that much less for her to take from him one day. If their marriage ended, she wanted to take everything she could get on the way out, and had set her sights on the château he loved. It would be doubly rewarding if she got it, because she knew how much he loved it. She wanted to hurt him as much as he had hurt her with the money he lost. She took it personally and was out for blood now. The last few years had been the worst of his life, with the humiliation of losing the business he had started and believed in so completely, and the worry of all the money he had lost, and being unable to find a comparable job to replace it. He was afraid that at fifty-six he was too old now, and his reputation had been tainted by the failure of the start-up. And being unemployed for three years was the greatest humiliation of all. He wasn't sorry he had launched his start-up, but he was desperately sorry it had failed. Global travel had died instantly in the pandemic and hadn't fully recovered yet.

He stopped several times on the road that night for coffee, in order to stay awake on the long drive. He had a meeting set up in Paris, trying to network for a job, and canceled it so he could be in Arcangues when the American woman came to see the château again. He was deeply protective of his ancestral home, and wanted to get a good look at her. He didn't like the idea of renting it for a year, or even six months, but if he got some income out of it, it would stall Brigitte for a while, and they could use the money. He intended to stay close by at the dower house to make sure that she wasn't damaging the property, or running it as an inn of some kind. The realtor had said he would discuss it all with her, and would bring a standard lease with him for her to sign if she agreed to Xavier's price and conditions.

Xavier finally got to Arcangues at two in the morning. He was exhausted and headed for his bedroom to sleep in his comfortable bed, maybe for the last time for a year. He didn't know how soon she wanted to move in. He walked to the main staircase in the dark, he knew the house perfectly, and tripped over the skateboard he had left there. It was an old one of Victoire's and he used it on the driveway sometimes to get to the far end quickly if he didn't want to drive. He'd forgotten he left it there, and reminded himself to put it away the next morning before the American woman came. There were a number of things he wanted to do, to make the château look inviting to her. He was running them all through his mind when he lay down on his bed a few minutes later. It was better than counting sheep. He fell asleep instantly, woke up at seven, and bounded out of bed to get started. He had a lot to do, starting with the skateboard he had fallen over the night before. Victoire had left it when she took the job in Africa. He liked seeing it to remind him of his daughter and happy times.

Chapter 6

S abrina left the Ritz at seven A.M. to catch an eight-
thirty flight to Biarritz from Orly. It was a short flight
and only took a little over an hour. They landed at nine-
forty. She had a cup of coffee at the airport, and there
was a car and driver waiting for her, arranged by the
concierge at the Ritz. She had a four P.M. flight back to
Paris. It was the only return flight she could get, but at
least she could conclude her business there in one day, if
there was business to conclude and she decided to rent
the château.

She wasn't sure how she'd feel about it seeing it for the
second time. Maybe she'd notice things she didn't like that
she hadn't observed before. Or the terms of the lease would
be unreasonable. The realtor had told her that the owner

wanted to meet her. She wondered if he was some old curmudgeon, but the skateboard she had noticed in the front hall was some indication that there was someone young in the house. There were only three bedrooms that were occupied. The others had white sheets over the furniture. The master suite was clearly occupied by a man and the second master by a woman, at opposite ends of the house so she didn't think they were a couple. And the other bedroom looked like it belonged to a young girl. The realtor had said that "the missus" was a doctor, and Sabrina wondered now if it was owned by three siblings who might all have to agree to the rental. She felt faintly nervous, as the driver took her on the road she'd been on before. And once in the village of Arcangues, she noticed the brilliant blue window shutters again. She loved the vibrant blue color and it made her want to paint them, an urge she hadn't had in a long time. She thought maybe she'd start painting again if she rented the château.

The realtor was waiting for her outside the main building, and the same caretaker she'd met before. He greeted her warmly, and they went through the house again. It looked tidier than on her first visit, and the skateboard and golf clubs were gone. The kitchen was immaculate. All three occupied bedrooms upstairs were in good order, and she noticed that there were vases of flowers in the living room, which gave life to the room. The house had been aired and smelled fresh, and it was a beautiful sunny day.

She liked the château even better than she had before. It felt warmer and more inviting. It was someone else's house but she had the odd feeling that she had come home. It made no sense, but there was an aura of peace in the house as she walked from room to room. It was much more space than she needed, with three wonderful bedrooms for all three of her children, and several additional ones for their friends. It was a home that would welcome house parties, and the gardens would lend themselves perfectly for entertaining in warm weather. And at the same time, she had the sense that she wouldn't mind being in the house alone. It didn't feel lonely or scary, and there were sconces throughout the main floor for candles. She found herself thinking that the original owners of the house must have given some beautiful dances. It had obviously belonged to nobility or very high aristocracy, and she wondered if Napoleon III and the Empress Eugénie had ever been there when they spent summers in the palace in Biarritz.

She was thinking of it when she walked into the kitchen and saw a tall, dark-haired man looking seriously at her, leaning against an antique wooden armoire used for dishes. She hadn't noticed him at first and gave a start. He advanced toward her and held out his hand to shake hers. He seemed very formal, and she noticed that he had sad eyes. He observed in the same instant that she did too. They were two very serious-looking people, and the caretaker and the realtor walked outside and left them alone to discuss business and the terms of a lease. Maxime and the realtor walked to a corner of the garden and sat down in the sun on a bench, and both lit cigarettes.

"Thank you for coming all the way from Paris, Mrs. Thompson," Xavier said formally. He had an accent, but she could tell he spoke fluent English, which was far better than her French. She was going to try to improve it if she rented the château.

"I wanted to see the house again, to be sure I wasn't making a mistake. You have a beautiful home," she said warmly, as a smile slowly lit her face. She was a little unnerved by how handsome he was. He looked to be around fifty. She wasn't sure what she had expected, but not someone close to her own age and who looked like him. He was movie star, ruggedly handsome, wearing jeans, a light blue shirt, a tweed jacket that looked very English, and riding boots. He had noticeable style, a thick head of dark hair peppered with gray, and a few lines around his eyes. He was a very good-looking man.

"Thank you. This château means a great deal to me. It's been in my family for three hundred years." He looked very dignified as he said it. And he clearly didn't take the responsibility lightly. "I've never rented it before. It's not for sale, but the realtor said you might want to rent it. Do you know this part of France well?" He was curious about her. She was wearing jeans too, with a chic black sweater, a warm black jacket trimmed with shearling, and fur-lined black Hermès boots. It was obvious from her clothes and her style that she had money, but she seemed very discreet. She had long blonde hair and had worn no makeup. There was no artifice about her, or pretentiousness. She seemed very modest and soft-spoken. There was a gentleness about her that suggested to him that she was a kind person. She didn't smile easily and he thought she looked sad.

"Actually, I came to Biarritz for the first time a few days ago. We . . . I . . . usually go to the south of France in the summer. I've never been to the Pays Basque before," she answered. "I drove down from Paris, and fell in love with Arcangues as soon as I saw it. The blue shutters are wonderful." As she said it, she smiled and so did he.

"That blue belongs exclusively to Arcangues. It was granted by the governors to the founder of the village, the Marquis d'Arcangues. The Château d'Arcangues was his. He was granted the exclusive use of that particular blue. He was a distant cousin of my father's, and my ancestors built this château to be near him. He was more illustrious than my relatives, and of higher rank, mine were only lowly barons, but families stayed close to each other in those days. So you can see I have close ties to this village." She could also see why he wouldn't sell it. "We stayed here during the pandemic to get away from Paris during the lockdowns. It was more pleasant being here than in the city. The confinement didn't change things much for us here. Or rather, I was here, my wife is a physician, and she was in Paris saving lives while I was working in the gardens." He smiled at her, and she liked him. She noticed that he wore a narrow wedding band, and she remembered that there were no women's clothes in the dressing room of the master suite, only his. The only women's clothes were at the opposite end of the château. There was obviously a story there of some kind. "I'm here a great deal of the time," he said. "I haven't moved back to Paris yet, but I'll go back to work there at some point." It was an interesting comment, since the pandemic had ended two years before. Clearly, he didn't live full-time with his wife. "Our daughter works in Africa, so I'm here alone most of the time. My wife isn't fond of country life. I won't be in your way, even when I'm here, but I would like to retain use of the dower house if you rent the château. The rest of the grounds would be for your use too. I'd like to be able to supervise the maintenance of the grounds, and I enjoy doing repairs on the property myself. I've become the château handyman. In fact, there are a number of small repairs I'd want to do before you take up residence. I've started a list." He pointed to a clipboard he had left on the kitchen table, and the list didn't look short to her. "You don't notice things when you're here all the time, or you put them off. I'd like to get all those little repairs fixed for you before you come to stay." He had told the realtor he would do no repairs for a tenant, but once he saw her he felt differently. She was a woman of quality and appeared to be alone, and there was something touching about her. "Will you be staying here full-time or only for holidays?" She hesitated before she answered, not sure what to say.

"To be honest, I don't know yet. I was looking for an apartment to buy in Paris, but I didn't find anything I liked, and then I drove down here on a whim, and fell in love. It's a new love affair for me." She smiled at him. "And if you'll forgive me for saying so, I immediately felt at home at the château. At first I thought I'd like to buy it, but knowing more now, I understand your not wanting to sell. And renting it for a year seemed like an interesting idea. I think I'd like to stay for a while. I live in L.A. and I have an art gallery there, but my children all live in other places, and I have no reason to rush back." She hesitated and then went on. "I lost my husband a few months ago. I'm still adjusting to the change," she said, and he suddenly understood the look in her eyes. She was a young woman to be widowed. She looked tragic for an instant as she said it.

"I'm so sorry. I understand. It must be a very big adjustment."

"It is," she confirmed softly, and then smiled at him. "And Arcangues seems like a much gentler place to do it than L.A. It was very sudden. He was ill for three months and then he died, last summer." So it was very fresh.

"This area is said to have healing properties, and this town in particular, and the church. I always come here when I need to soothe my soul," Xavier said gently. "I think you'd be happy here," he ventured to say.

"I think so too," she said in her soft voice and didn't push him, and he suddenly liked the idea of her being there, and wondered if they'd become friends. She seemed very bright and interesting, despite her soft voice and gentle ways. He could tell that her husband had been a great loss from the way she spoke of him and his sudden death. "It's such a beautiful area," she said, and he smiled warmly as she said it.

"There's nothing like it anywhere in the world. Biarritz is fun, and the palace must have been outrageous when it was built. But there is something very special and unusual about this village. You said your children live in other places.

Are they in Europe?" He was increasingly curious about her, beyond the rental of his home.

"My children are all over the place now. My son is in London, I have a daughter in law school in New York, and a daughter working for Prada in Milan."

"My daughter is a nurse practitioner in a refugee camp in Zimbabwe."

"She must be a remarkable woman."

"I think so," Xavier said proudly. "Her mother is a doctor, from a medical family, three generations of doctors. And her maternal grandmother was a nurse. It's in their blood, though not in mine, I'm afraid. My daughter hasn't been home in two years because of the pandemic. I visited her last year in Zimbabwe. I'm hoping she'll come for a visit soon, but she loves her work and is very dedicated."

"Two of mine are just finishing graduate school, and the one in Milan is in her first job. They've all flown the nest. My husband and I were going to travel. He was going to retire in two years, but all those plans changed. Now I'm trying to figure out the next steps, without my husband or my kids. It's a big change." Sabrina tried to sound philosophical about it.

"This would be a good place to figure that out."

"That's how I felt when I saw it," she said, looking young and vulnerable. He guessed her to be about ten years younger than he was, but she was forty-eight. And it sounded and looked as though she had been through a lot.

"And you wouldn't mind my living on the property?" he asked her.

"Not at all," she said warmly. "This is your home. I'm the intruder, but I'll try to be a discreet one."

"I'm an excellent handyman," he said with a broad smile, and she tried not to notice how good-looking he was. He was a married man, which she respected, and she wasn't flirting with him, but it was hard not to notice his looks. He had noticed hers as well, and thought she looked more European than American. "Would you like to take a walk in the gardens? There are some secret paths you might enjoy."

"I'd like that," Sabrina said shyly, and followed him outside.

"I keep two horses here as well, they're very old and steady. You're welcome to ride them whenever you want." He led her to the entrance to the gardens, and along some very pretty hidden paths. Some had been designed with the house. They sat on a bench in the sun in one of them, and he was surprised by how easy she was to talk to. She was a gentle person. There was nothing sharp or strident about her. It struck him how different she was from Brigitte. Sabrina seemed to be the exact opposite. Brigitte competed with men, and tried to subjugate and diminish them. Sabrina had a light, gentle touch that made a man feel strong and want to protect her. She seemed vulnerable, and kind. She reminded him that there were decent women in the world. Brigitte had wounded him deeply for years.

They walked slowly back to the house after an hour, and he looked at her as they stood in the main garden. Two gardeners were working nearby. They were Basques and had strong Spanish features and were speaking to each other in dialect.

"Well, Mrs. Thompson, do we meet with your approval?" he asked her, and she looked surprised.

"Do I? I got the impression that you wanted to check me out to make sure I wasn't some brash American who was going to paint the château pink or fly an American flag on the front lawn." He laughed because it was true, but she was the opposite of what he had expected. And she hadn't complained about the rent. He was embarrassed now at the price he had quoted the realtor, which he thought was too much and she thought was a bargain. And she hadn't said a word about it.

"Perhaps we were both being cautious," he said.

"There's nothing wrong with that," she said.

"When would you want to occupy it?" It all seemed very sudden and she hadn't given it any thought.

"I'm staying in Paris now, at a hotel. Soon would be nice, but I understand that this is sudden for both of us. Would two weeks be too soon?"

"I think I can do all the minor repairs I have in mind by then," he said. "Is that too long a wait for you, staying at a hotel?" he asked her, and she smiled.

"I think I can find some things to occupy me. I'm addicted to museums and art galleries, and there are more than enough to keep me busy for two weeks." He suggested the first of February and she agreed. She inquired about a security deposit, which she expected to be a large amount, and he said one month was sufficient. He gave her his bank details to wire that and the first month's rent. He showed her the simple lease form the realtor had given him. It was extremely basic, and he asked if she wanted an attorney to review it, and she said she didn't. There was no small print, it was straightforward and clear. They both signed two copies of it, shook hands, and the Château de Bonport was her home for the next year, however much she wished to use it. It was the easiest transaction either of them had ever made. He walked her to her car, and she slid into the back seat as Xavier leaned down to smile at her and spoke softly. The driver and Maxime were talking and not paying attention.

"Welcome home, Mrs. Thompson. I hope you'll be happy here."

"I'm sure I will, Monsieur de Bonport. Or is it Baron?" She looked confused for a minute as she said it, and he laughed.

"It's Xavier," he said firmly, still smiling.

"It's Sabrina. See you in two weeks, and thank you for trusting me with your wonderful house. I promise I'll be good to it."

"I know you will. And you won't even know I'm here. I will be the country mouse at the dower house. *Au revoir,* Sabrina, until soon."

She waved as they drove away. She was smiling. She had a château in France for a year. It was the craziest thing she'd ever done. The realtor met her at his office and made a copy of the signed lease. Xavier was paying the commission, and the realtor couldn't believe how smoothly it had gone. He shook hands with Sabrina and told her to call him if she had any problems, and then she took off for the airport. It was already two o'clock, and she had to check in at three. She had a sandwich at the airport, and boarded the plane. They landed at Orly at five o'clock, and she was back at the Ritz at six. She called all the children to tell them what she'd done. And they thought it was a little crazy too, but they were all so relieved that she was coming to life again and excited about the château. They all agreed to spend their vacation there that summer instead of the south of France. It was a new adventure that she had embarked on without Malcolm. It was bittersweet because it was confirmation that he was never coming back. And she wondered if she and Baron Xavier de Bonport would become friends. He said he was going back to Paris to work in the coming months, but she got the feeling that he couldn't stay away from Arcangues for long, and it would be nice to have someone to talk to from time to time. She'd enjoyed meeting him. He seemed like a good person, and he had thought the same about her.

Brigitte called him that night, wanting to know how the meeting had gone.

"Was she awful?" she asked, curious about Sabrina.

"Not at all. She's a very polite, proper widow."

"What does she want with a château in the Pays Basque?"

"She just lost her husband and I think she's still in deep mourning for him, and came here to recover. Some people like it here."

"How depressing." Brigitte dismissed her, and never asked how old she was or if she was good-looking. Xavier would have told her the truth, he always did, but she didn't ask or care. "Did she rent it?"

"Yes, for a year."

"For how much?" He told her and she was stunned. It was a very healthy sum that would more than pay their bills every month. There was nothing to complain about there. "Maybe she would buy it from you at a big price. That might make you reconsider," she said hopefully.

"No, it wouldn't," he said firmly. They hung up a few minutes later. Neither of them had anything else to say.

Sabrina kept busy in Paris with all the things she liked to do when she was there. All of them brought back haunting memories of Malcolm, and she worked through each of them day by day. She went to all her favorite museums, wandered down all the streets on the Left Bank where the galleries she liked best were, walked in the Luxembourg Gardens and the Bois de Boulogne and Bagatelle, shopped on the Avenue Montaigne and the Faubourg Saint-Honoré for her daughters, and even bought a few things for herself. She felt as though she was waking up from long, dark months, and had been in a daze. She didn't like going to restaurants alone, so on most evenings she had room service in her suite at the Ritz, but by then she was tired from walking miles all over Paris and was happy to be tucked in, reading art books she bought at the museums she went to.

She flew to Biarritz on the first of February. She had been speaking to at least one of her children every day, and they were excited for her to be taking possession of the château and were eager to see it. They had decided that it would be good for her. She bought a car in Biarritz, so she could get around with ease. And she had bought some pretty sheets at Porthault to use for her bed at the Château de Bonport. The realtor had assured her that the house came with linens, but she was particular about her own. Malcolm had always commented on the beautiful sheets she bought for their bed. And even if no one else saw them now, she enjoyed them too. She hadn't brought many clothes and only had two suitcases with her, but she had added a few things in Paris. She didn't expect to need anything fancy at the château, and if she needed more, Hallie could go through her closets in Malibu and send her what she was missing.

Maxime the caretaker helped her with her bags when she arrived, and two cartons of art books she had brought. She settled in quickly. She went to the local market and cooked her first meal in the kitchen. She noticed a number of things that her landlord had repaired or replaced, and smiled when she saw that the brass knocker on the front door had been shined until it gleamed. She didn't see Xavier de Bonport when she arrived, and didn't ask if he was there. She didn't want to be nosy or intrusive.

She arrived on a Friday, spent Saturday settling in, and went to Biarritz to pick up the car. It was a little red Fiat, which was all she needed to get around. If she went on any long trips, she could rent a larger car, but she had no plans to travel at the moment.

Maxime's wife cleaned the château once a week, and he found her two young local girls to clean and do laundry every weekday. Sabrina was going to cook for herself every night and make her own bed on the weekends. She spoke to the two girls in her awkward French.

And on Sunday morning, she decided to attend the choir mass at the monastery that the realtor had told her about.

She sat in a pew at the rear of the church, and closed her eyes as she listened to the music. The voices were exquisite. There were about forty children staying at the convent, and some of the local children had joined the choir. Their voices were beautiful, like angels, blending with the nuns'.

She lit a candle for Malcolm and for each of her children, which was a Catholic practice she had always loved ever since she was a child, although she was baptized Episcopalian. She was a frequent churchgoer but not a constant one, and she liked the service at the monastery. She was leaving the church when she saw Xavier de Bonport alone on the steps, leaving just ahead of her. He turned as she approached him, and was surprised to see her. He smiled at her, and seemed pleased.

"Did you find everything in good order?" he asked her.

"Perfectly. Thank you for fixing so many things, and for

the new toaster and microwave," she commented, and he laughed.

"My wife doesn't believe in them and thinks they're unhealthy. But I thought you might want them." She had tried the microwave the night before and the toaster that morning.

"I've already used them," she confirmed. "You must have been busy."

"I got it all done in a week," he said proudly. "I had meetings in Paris this week. I got back last night. I saw the lights on but didn't want to bother you."

"The front door knocker looks gorgeous, by the way," she said, as he walked her to her new car.

"I polished it myself. It's original with the house. It shined up very nicely." He looked relaxed and happy as they chatted. "I like your new car."

"I bought it yesterday in Biarritz," she said, smiling at him.

"I ride a bicycle here most of the time. I walked this morning."

"Would you like a ride home?" she offered.

"That would be very nice, thank you."

She asked him about a marina or yacht club, on the way back, and he told her about the two closest ports half an hour away. They were Anglet and Ciboure harbors, and they weren't fancy.

"Are you buying a boat too?" he asked, impressed, and wondered if she was planning to buy a large yacht. He had the feeling that she had unlimited money to spend, she had been so easy about the rent. He assumed that she had just inherited a fortune from her husband, and was spending it liberally. In fact, she hadn't touched a penny of what Malcolm had left her. It was all invested. The money she was spending was all her own.

"My husband had a beautiful sailboat he loved. It's very old and quite lovely. I took it out of the water this winter. No one's used it since . . ." Her voice trailed off for an instant, and she went on. "I thought it would be nice for the children to have it here this summer. I want to get it shipped over. It's not a very big boat, and they love it. It will be fun for them here. They're all good sailors and love his boat." She was definitely settling in, and when they got out at the château, he hesitated for a minute, and then decided to brave it.

"There's a very nice quiet, simple restaurant in Biarritz I thought you might like. I wanted to invite you to dinner to thank you for renting the château. It solves some problems for me, and you've been so nice about everything. Would you like to have dinner there tomorrow night?" She was startled by the invitation, but touched that he had asked her. It was unexpected and generous, and she was moved too by his admission of problems. She wondered if that accounted for the melancholy look in his eyes at times. There was something troubling him, but she had no idea what it was. Maybe the wife in Paris who hated Arcangues and had her own bedroom far from his. It was a rather obvious clue when she had seen their sleeping arrangements. All their clothes had been packed up and removed, and their daughter's, to get the house ready for Sabrina and her family.

"That sounds lovely," Sabrina answered him about dinner. "You'll have to come to the main house for dinner one night. I saw some wonderful langoustines at the market."

"My favorite." He smiled at her. He was enjoying the banter, and she looked very pretty in a simple white sweater and blue jeans and a parka she had bought in Paris. The parka was almost the same special blue as the shutters in Arcangues, which was why she had bought it. The similarity of color had struck him too. "That's our blue," Xavier said, and she nodded, shy for a minute.

"It's so bright and alive and vibrant," she said, "and so hopeful. It's the color of hope," she added, smiling at him.

"We all need a bit of that, don't we," he said, as a cloud came over his eyes again. "The color of hope. I like that."

"So do I," she said thoughtfully.

"I'll pick you up at eight tomorrow. Does that work for you?" he asked her, and she laughed.

"I'll have to check, I'm terribly busy. I have appointments all day, dinner parties every night, and business lunches," she said, and he laughed too. She had a light touch and he liked that about her. He could see that she had weathered a heavy storm, but she could still laugh, and smile, and be kind to him. *"À demain,"* she said in French . . . till tomorrow . . . as he walked briskly back to the dower house. It was cold out, but he was smiling as he waved, and so was she when she walked into the château and gently closed the heavy door with the brass knocker. It had been nice seeing him at church. It made her feel like a local and as though she belonged there. She was looking forward to dinner with him the next day. For an instant she questioned her own motives. He was married, after all, and she was mourning Malcolm, but it was nice to know someone in the village. She decided that it was all right, and she didn't need to feel guilty. There were no ulterior motives on either side. Just two people being kind to each other, and needing a friend to talk to. It was harmless.

Chapter 7

Xavier de Bonport picked up Sabrina at eight o'clock right on time, as promised. She had noticed that about him before, that he was punctual and precise, and he did what he promised. He was a man of his word.

He was dressed simply, but had a distinctive style. He wasn't showy or pretentious. He was wearing black jeans, a black turtleneck, a black leather jacket that was well worn, and impeccably shined black leather John Lobb shoes. He and Sabrina almost looked like twins. She was wearing identical jeans and sweater and an old Balenciaga black leather coat, an exact copy of one Audrey Hepburn had worn in one of her films. Her father had had many of Audrey Hepburn's films as part of his library, and Sabrina had watched them again and again and had adopted several of her signature styles. Sabrina and Xavier made a handsome couple as she got in his unassuming old Citroën and they headed toward Biarritz. The restaurant he had chosen was on a narrow back street and looked plain from the outside, but the atmosphere was lively and fun inside, and they had delicious Basque food. Sabrina had been reading about the region, and was intrigued by many of the local traditions and ties to Spain. She was planning to drive around the area when the weather got better. She and Malcolm had loved learning about local culture on their many trips to France. She knew he would have loved Arcangues. And the people in the shops were friendly to her and patient with her French.

Xavier made some suggestions of what to eat, and Sabrina followed his advice. The food was excellent and she loved it.

"Thank you for taking me to dinner," she said after the first course, as they shared some delicious homemade bread. The cook and owner of the restaurant was a large woman who looked like a grandmother and went from table to table several times during the evening to make sure that everyone was loving the food. They always did, and Sabrina was enjoying the ambiance and Xavier's company. His eyes were bright that night. He had talked about his daughter and how proud of her he was, and how much he missed her.

"The pandemic has disconnected us all," he said, "from our families, our loved ones, our friends, our coworkers. That was one of the biggest impacts it had on me. It made us solitary. I find it hard to reconnect to people, especially as I'm here, and not in Paris, working," although it was certainly not a bad place to live in exile.

"Are you working remotely?" she asked him. She had no idea what his job was, and didn't want to be presumptuous and ask. He gave her the sense that he was a very private person, and he had an air of quiet dignity. She could guess that he was a proud man, a well-known trait of the Basques that she was reading avidly about.

He hesitated before he answered her question. "I'm not really working," he said humbly. "I haven't in three years. I made a daring gamble with a new business, the pandemic hit, and a year and a half later, I lost. Everything." He said it without shame, and didn't hide it, but she could see pain and regret in his eyes. "It was a global travel business, a start-up, connecting every aspect of travel globally. The pandemic hit, the frontiers closed, every country shut down, and travel ended. We called it Bon Voyage. It was a great idea and the pandemic killed it. We couldn't save it. We lost the business. You bought me time and peace, by renting the château." He didn't look as though he needed the money, but she had wondered why he had rented a home he was so intensely attached to. He didn't try to hide the truth from her or put on airs. He was very open and direct and brave about it. He didn't want to start a friendship with her on false pretenses. He was an honest man.

"I was the head of a big ad agency in Paris for twenty years before that. It was a great job, greater than I knew at the time. But I fell in love with the idea of a global start-up based on travel. Perhaps the right idea at the wrong time. No one could have predicted the pandemic, and the entire world shut down. The idea was sound, but the timing was terrible. We had the worst luck in the world. When everything had become global, suddenly the entire planet stopped, countries closed their borders, no one could travel, alliances between companies and countries were severed, and panic reigned. We tried to ride it out, but we couldn't. We had it going full speed in the year before the pandemic, and it was headed to a huge success, which evaporated in our hands from the moment the pandemic hit. I had given up a very big job to do it, and invested too much personal money in it. One of my associates had a large fortune to draw on, and it was a lark to him. He died in the first month of the pandemic, which hit us hard, personally and practically. I had taken a huge risk and poured everything I had into the business, I was so sure it would work. The third partner was a brilliant technician, and had very little money to put in. He lost his wife and his interest in everything, including our business. He had five children and he's only now starting to see clearly again more than three years later. He just remarried, and they moved to the Dominican Republic. We had too many hard hits between one partner's death, the other one losing his wife, and me losing all my money. I think we would have won the bet and made billions without the pandemic, but with it we were doomed. Or maybe the project was too ambitious, and the time for dreams and castles in the air is past. Travel is still very fragile now." He was being totally honest with her. "I lay low for a year after we closed, licking my wounds. I assumed I'd go back to a big job like the one I had before in advertising, but I think I was too old, or had demonstrated instability in some people's eyes when I quit to start a new business with a global concept. I thought I'd be the CEO of a large company again, after the pandemic, after the business failed. I thought that finding a job as a CEO again would be easy and always available to me. I was fifty-three when we dissolved the start-up. I'm fifty-six now, almost fifty-seven, and that's a dicey age. People don't want to invest in you or hire you if they're only going to get five or ten years out of you at most. Or maybe what I tried to do was too crazy, or no one trusted me to be steadfast anymore, once I quit my big job. The pandemic ended two years ago and I haven't landed a job. There are jobs out there but they're going to younger men. The whole concept of work is different. People have realized too that they don't want to sacrifice their whole lives to their jobs, which is what I did for my entire career. After spending two years at home, gardening and getting to know their children, whom they had never spent any time with, now people don't want to go back to a traditional office. And the simple fact is that younger men are cheaper to hire than I am. Overnight I became a dinosaur, along with many traditional businesses. Corporations have disbanded their offices, commercial buildings are empty, and the young workforce is at home in their pajamas and playing with their dog. They've moved out of the cities, so it's damn hard to put a functioning work team together, particularly with younger people who think we've destroyed the planet and their lives. And classic, highly paid CEOs like me have gone out of style. We blinked and a whole world ended and the life that went with it. In some ways, I like it better too. I'm happier here in Arcangues where I grew up than I ever was in Paris. The trouble is that I need the kind of salary I had to maintain that lifestyle, and I spent everything I'd saved on a start-up that failed. I could be a gardener," he said, smiling wryly at her, "or a carpenter, but I doubt that I'll be a CEO again, and my entire life and professional structure was based on that.

Young people and investors don't trust that model anymore. So I've retreated to my land, like a feudal 'seigneur,' a lord, but I don't have the fortune to support it. All I have left is the château, and I'm hanging on to it for dear life for my daughter. You helped me do that when you rented it. You gave me time and breathing space to figure out what I'm going to do now. The world has changed, and we all have to adapt," he said nobly, but now she better understood the sadness she had seen in his eyes. He was a proud man, and in his eyes, and perhaps the world's, he had failed, not through his own fault, but the story wasn't over yet.

"What does your wife say?" she asked, curious about her. "I gather she's not in love with the idea of moving to the Pays Basque," since she wasn't there with him, and the separate bedrooms Sabrina had noticed when she first toured the house told their own tale.

"She can't. She has a serious medical practice, tied to a teaching hospital. She has an important job, although it pays almost nothing. She's in Public Health. Our life and the lifestyle she came to enjoy relied on me, and I've let her down. Fortunately, we have an undemanding daughter who does the work of angels in a refugee camp. The pandemic changed everything for most people. It put everything under a microscope in the spotlight. Whatever was wrong before is in question now, or has simply been thrown away. A lot of things should have been. Relationships and marriages that had survived for years with accommodations and arrangements and were only a front for what lay behind them no longer make any sense.

"This is a time for truth and reality, not fakery and pretense. Brigitte and I never had a good marriage. We were a mistake for a good cause. We dated for a short time, were unsuited to each other. I'm a royalist, if you want to call it that, a remnant of a social structure that doesn't exist anymore, a lifestyle and career built on capitalism, big showy jobs for big money. The perks are nice, but a lot of what held that together was empty and has crumbled. She's an extreme socialist, which is the world in which she grew up and works now. She believes in it profoundly. She hated everything I stood for, but the prestige and benefits compensated for having married the wrong man. I thought I was doing 'the right thing' when I married her, and I was willing to sacrifice my own dreams for her and our child, and our daughter is an incredible human being. She is the best of both of us, but she's not here anymore. She has her own life in Africa, which she loves. And we are left to face each other and ourselves, and the lies we told ourselves that it would all work out. It didn't, right from the beginning.

"She should have married a doctor, like her. It's the only world she respects, and men like her father. She has an insufferable brother, a big cardiac surgeon, but those are the men she respects. The only thing she ever liked about me was my success. Without that, she will resent me forever for the job I gave up, and the money I lost. Without that, I have nothing she wants. I sold our rather grand apartment to put some money back in the bank, and we have that, and now she wants to do the same with the château. But I can't, and I won't. The château is all about bloodlines and heritage and family. It's not about real estate or money. The decisions about its ultimate fate will be my daughter's, and her grandchildren's, not mine. I owe it to her to preserve it for her." He had deeply rooted family values, which touched Sabrina, and she was sorry to hear that he'd been through such a hard time. She understood the dilemma and the reasons for the separate bedrooms now.

"By renting the château, you gave me a year of grace to figure out my future, and a reliable income to replace my job. That's an enormous gift. I'm sorry to tell you my sad stories. They aren't really. They're technicalities, and details, but a lot rests on those details. If I'm never going to be a CEO again, I need to figure out who I will be. I'd love to do another start-up, but I don't have the funds anymore, and I'm not sure I ever will again. And I'd need faith in myself to do that, and I seem to have lost some confidence, for now at least. No one is going to invest in a man with poor judgment, who threw a golden job away, and who has already failed once."

"It sounds like the pandemic did you in, not poor judgment," she said, touched by all that he had shared with her so openly and honestly.

"I didn't want you to think that I was some snob with his château, swanning around and showing off. I'm really no more than a tenant there now myself. The château is valuable, but for much deeper reasons than my wife recognizes, or ever will."

"Would you ever get divorced?" she asked cautiously, as it seemed to be much more part of the American culture than the French one.

"I can't. The château is all I have now of any financial value. If we got divorced, I'd have to sell it and give her half. Technically, my daughter could oppose the sale, but she probably wouldn't win. My wife deserves something for thirty unhappy years."

"And what do you deserve, Xavier?" she asked him quietly. It was an important question, maybe the most important. She could see easily how guilty he felt about the job he'd given up, and the money he had lost, and felt a moral responsibility to pay penance for it.

"I certainly don't deserve a reward for the mistakes I made."

"You didn't cause the pandemic."

"I shouldn't have risked everything on the start-up. I thought it was a sure thing, so I invested everything I had. That was a mistake. We probably would have made billions if the pandemic hadn't hit. Instead, we lost it all."

"You're not the first human being to make that mistake, investing everything in something you believed in passionately. That's how fortunes are made."

"And lost," he added.

"We all do something like it at some point in our lives," Sabrina said kindly, "whether it's a job or a marriage, or a house or a friendship. Life involves risk, and sometimes you lose."

"I've noticed," he said with a rueful smile. "My wife and I had things worked out so we spent very little time together when I ran the ad agency. And she basically lived at the hospital during the first year of the pandemic. Now I stay down here to avoid her, and I only go to Paris for meetings for job opportunities. We rented a ridiculous apartment, which is more like a storage unit. It's too small for both of us, and there is only one topic of conversation between us, selling the château. I will never forgive myself if I do. And she'll never forgive me if I don't. Actually she will never forgive me anyway. She's a hard woman. And she has strong family support. They think I'm an idiot because I'm not a doctor. They tolerated me as a CEO. That's over. I haven't seen them in two years, and try hard not to."

"Do you have other family?"

"Not anymore. My parents died a long time ago. My mother died when I was at university, and my father not long after. He was much older than my mother. He came from a world where people of good breeding didn't work. They owned their land, thought commerce was beneath them. My father was a banker, which was acceptable in his world. He was always embarrassed by my job and my success. He thought it was 'common.' I loved it. I find business exciting. If the start-up had worked, I'd still be up to my ears in it. I wish I were. I would take a much lesser job than the one I had, but people think I'm overqualified and would be bored and offended and wouldn't stay. I don't want to retire, I want to work for at least another twenty years."

"My husband wanted to retire. He made the decision at fifty to retire at fifty-five, so we could travel. He'd been in a high stress job all his life, and he'd had enough."

"What did he do?" Xavier asked. He wondered what kind of man she had been married to. He guessed a wealthy one. She had the quiet self-assurance of a woman who didn't need to worry about money, although she didn't show off and wasn't pretentious.

"He was the head of a television network. It was a very high-pressure job, and when our youngest daughter left for college, he realized that he wanted time for us. He died before we could do it."

Xavier was impressed by what she said. "Was it fun for you, his job?" he asked her.

"Sometimes. I never lived vicariously through his job, and I had been around Hollywood all my life, growing up. My father was a movie producer, and my mother was an actress when she was young. My father was older too."

"That must have been very interesting. What kind of movies did he produce?" She smiled and didn't dodge the question.

"Big ones," she said simply, and reeled off the names of a few that had been global hits and that he would know. Xavier looked startled. He knew them all, they were some of the all-time greats of Hollywood.

"My God, those are all major movies. Do you have brothers and sisters?" She shook her head.

"No, I'm an only child like you. And my parents died fairly young too. My father had a heart attack in his sixties. I didn't want that to happen to Malcolm, my husband. But in the end, it did anyway."

"A heart attack?"

"No." She explained about ALS, and he realized the hell

127

she had been through, watching him rapidly deteriorate. She had had her hard times too, but their marriage seemed to have been solid, unlike his with Brigitte.

"Was it a good marriage?" he asked her gently. She looked wistful for a minute, and spoke the truth.

"It was perfect. He was the right man at the right time for the right reasons. We were incredibly lucky. It really was a perfect marriage, and now he's gone. I have no idea what to do with the rest of my life, and I don't even live in the same city with any of my children. I don't want to encroach on them because I'm alone." He thought it was nice of her not to try to hang on to them, and he could see how solitary she was. She was trying to forge her own way alone, in a foreign country, in a totally unfamiliar world. He respected her a lot for trying to do that, and not just sitting at home, wrapped in her memories and feeling sorry for herself. She was a brave woman.

"I envy you. I can't even imagine that kind of marriage. Brigitte and I aren't even friends. It has made the past three years even harder."

"You'll find another job or a project, Xavier." He was energetic and dynamic, and intelligent. "The right thing will come along and surprise you when you least expect it."

"I used to think that too, but recently I've had my doubts. I don't see anything on the horizon."

"It will come. You're too young for this to be the end of your story. Either another big job, or another start-up. Which would you prefer?" She was curious about the answer. And he smiled.

"I'm not sure. I loved the prestige and power of my job as CEO. It made me feel important," he said honestly, hiding nothing from her. "But the start-up was much more fun. I'd love to do both again, or some kind of fun project. You had an art gallery, didn't you?" He vaguely remembered.

"I still do, and I had a terrific time with it. But nothing is fun now without Malcolm."

"You will find the right project too," he reassured her. She was still young, and smart and beautiful. He couldn't envision a woman like Sabrina doing nothing, just languishing in the château with no project or activity. She was too energetic to do that, even now.

When they left the restaurant, they'd both had a wonderful evening. They had bared their souls and been completely honest with each other, without artifice or secrets. Sabrina was entirely alone in France and needed a friend to talk to. She spoke to her children almost every day, but that wasn't the same thing. And she wanted to appear strong for them. She was their only parent now. Xavier needed someone he could confide in too, to balance the soul-crushing blows that Brigitte dealt him every time she told him what a loser he was. It was so obvious that she didn't like or respect him. He wondered now if she ever had. If so, it was so long ago that neither of them could remember it. All he remembered now was how bad it had been right from the beginning. Neither of them had been enthusiastic about getting married, but had done it for the baby she got pregnant with and to please their parents. A marriage like the one Sabrina described to Malcolm was completely foreign to him and Brigitte.

They walked for a little while after they left the restaurant. The dinner had been excellent, and it was fun seeing the nightlife of Biarritz for a few minutes. They stopped to look at the ocean and the boats in the distance.

"I had a terrific evening," he said to her. "I'm sorry to tell you all that unhappy history, and the start-up and all of it."

"It's part of your life, it's real. These things happen to people, marriages go sour, businesses fail, kids get into trouble, people we love get sick and die. It's all part of life." She was more philosophical about her losses and heartbreaks than he was. He was still railing at the fates and fighting with Brigitte. Sabrina seemed to have risen above the tragedies and disappointments in her life. "Life is scary sometimes, and sad. It's easier to get through if there are two of you. I always had Malcolm to protect me and face anything hard with me. It doesn't sound like you had that with Brigitte."

"Certainly not," he confirmed. "She's not a supportive person. She is very competitive, especially with men. I think at times she wanted to be me, not be married to me." Sabrina thought it was an interesting observation and wondered if he was right.

He dropped her off at the château and watched her go in. It was an odd feeling watching her go into his house, and he wasn't living there. And all he could think as he drove to the dower house was what a good friend she could be, and he hoped that eventually, she would be. Even knowing her for a short time, he trusted her completely, and she trusted him. It was a good place to start.

The day after Sabrina's dinner with Xavier, she sent him a friendly text, thanking him for a wonderful evening, and after she sent it, she dressed and drove to the monastery. She wanted to look around and see what they did there. Xavier had spoken highly of the nuns there at dinner the night before. It made her want to at least meet them. They were neighbors, after all.

She rang the bell at the outer gate, and a very elderly nun opened the door in the wall. Sabrina was surprised by how big the inner courtyard was, and the convent garden.

It seemed much smaller when viewed from outside. It looked like a busy village and a world unto itself. It was in an old fortress, with the church right next door where she had gone to mass on Sunday.

"May I help you?" the nun who was the doorkeeper on duty asked her with a wide smile. She looked to be somewhere in her eighties and walked with a cane but she was very spry.

"Am I allowed to take a look around, Sister?" Sabrina asked.

"Of course," the elderly nun said warmly. "The walls are here to shelter us, not to keep anyone out." Sabrina noticed nuns leading groups of children to what looked like classrooms. There were dormitories as well, and she noticed that there were both boys and girls at the monastery, of all ages. There were the sounds of talking and laughter, and a few squeals from the children, and now and then one child would break from the group and run around. There was a beautiful garden with benches, and a separate vegetable garden where two nuns were putting what it produced into baskets. When they finished, one of them came over to speak to Sabrina on the bench. Sabrina had been fascinated by the methodical project. They were Dominican nuns, each in the white habit of the order with a black veil. Sabrina was intrigued to see that they hadn't modernized their habits, which were still long, with wide sleeves. Large wooden rosaries hung from the nuns' waists, and they were all wearing sandals barefoot, even in winter. She noticed that they had sweet faces, and the nun who approached her was smiling and came to sit down next to her. It was difficult to guess her age. Sabrina thought maybe somewhere in her thirties.

"Are you traveling?" she asked Sabrina kindly in English. She was wearing her favorite blue parka.

"No, Sister. I just moved in, at the Château de Bonport."

"Then we're neighbors. I'm Sister Anne. I'm in charge of the school here." Sabrina was intrigued by how lively the inner courtyard of the convent was. It seemed like a happy place, and the children looked neat and well cared for. Many of them were young, but a handful were in their teens.

"How many children are there here?"

"Forty-seven," Sister Anne said proudly. "We actually have room for thirty-five, but the diocese always sends us a few extras. We have more than usual right now, it's not normally this crowded."

"Is it an orphanage?" Sabrina asked her.

"No, though some of the children are orphans, some because of the pandemic, or from other circumstances. It's a temporary home, until we can assess their situations, and place them appropriately. Many of them will go to foster homes when they leave here. Others will stay with us until their parents can come back for them, if they are in some kind of transition and can't care for them right now, but can eventually. In some cases, we're looking for their parents, and their status as to whether they qualify for adoption or foster care, if it hasn't been determined. We research each child very carefully, so we don't make any mistakes. The four teenagers over there are here until they turn eighteen in a few months, and we'll try to place them in the community and help them find jobs. Sometimes they live with families in the area until they get on their feet."

"It sounds like a very efficient operation," Sabrina said with admiration. And a compassionate one, designed to meet the children's needs.

"We try to be," Sister Anne said. Sabrina introduced herself then. "Do you sing, Sabrina?" Sister Anne asked kindly, and Sabrina laughed.

"Not a note."

"You're welcome to try out for the chorus. We can always use fresh voices. And you're welcome to visit the children any time. It's good for them to see people who aren't nuns. Many of them are very shy. They've had hard experiences before they got here. We try to help them get over it."

Sabrina wondered if they got therapy for their hard experiences, or just religious training, but she didn't want to ask. "We dine at five-thirty every day, and there's always a spare meal at our table." She was so hospitable that it made Sabrina want to stay forever. The atmosphere inside the convent walls felt like a blessing, and she liked Sister Anne immensely.

"Our Mother Superior is very modern in her thinking," Sister Anne explained to Sabrina. "And the Provincial of the Order sends us children from all over France. There are other interim residences like us, but children seem to like to come here." She looked at Sabrina seriously for a minute then. "Do you know the history of the Château de Bonport?" she asked her.

"Very little. Just what the owner told me."

"Ah yes, Mr. de Bonport. He's very helpful to us. He volunteers to lend us a hand whenever he's here. He's very handy with a hammer and nails and a wrench. We have a handyman here but he's very old now. So Mr. de Bonport does whatever he can. I was referring to the history from the last war."

"He hasn't told me," Sabrina answered.

"He should. His grandmother was a very brave woman. Xavier de Bonport's grandfather was shot and killed in the Resistance. He was quite young, his son was only three, and the baroness was in her twenties. They built underground tunnels and passages to hide Jewish children when the Nazis started rounding them up. They had a very efficient system to erase all trace of them, give them new identities, and get them out of France. Apparently, she was fearless, and they saved close to a thousand children, right under the noses of the German soldiers billeted at the Château de Bonport. The senior officers and headquarters were at the Château d'Arcangues, but the whole rescue operation was underground at Bonport. It's quite a beautiful story, isn't it? That was his grandmother. His family has a long history of helping the villagers. I'm surprised he hasn't told you. You should ask him about it. He's a very modest person."

"Yes, he is," Sabrina agreed. She was fascinated by the story.

"Well, I've got to get my vegetables to the kitchen for tonight's dinner. It's my turn in the vegetable garden. We rotate." There were eighteen nuns in residence, she had told Sabrina, and forty-seven children. That was sixty-five people they were feeding at every meal. That was a lot of people.

Sabrina couldn't wait to ask Xavier about his grandmother the next time she saw him.

She thought about the nuns and the convent and the

children on her way back to the château. Going there had made her want to volunteer there too. She wasn't handy with a hammer like Xavier, but maybe she could play with the children, or help serve meals. It would be a nice way to spend her time, and she missed having children around. She was planning to go back and ask Sister Anne about it. She wondered if the secret tunnels and passages were still underground at the château. It was an impressive story, for a young woman with a three-year-old herself at the time, after her husband was shot in the Resistance. It made Sabrina think that one antidote for her grief might be helping others, not as dramatically as Xavier's grandmother, but where there were children, there was always work to do. And she had plenty of time to do it.

Chapter 8

S abrina went back to visit the monastery again a few days later. It was officially called St. Steven's, but everyone just called it the monastery. She hadn't seen Xavier since they had dinner, so she hadn't been able to ask him about his grandmother's wartime activities, or if the tunnels were still intact under the château. She spoke to Sister Anne about volunteering, and the nun welcomed the idea, and introduced her to Mother Regina, the Mother Superior, who was a tiny little woman with what appeared to be boundless energy and a will of iron, and who, Sister Anne told Sabrina afterward, was eighty-five. She looked sixty.

Sabrina found it comforting to be among the nuns. There was a strong sense of community and productive activity, and the children reminded her of when her own children were young, and made her smile and laugh. She played games with them, and even got roped into one of their soccer matches on the front lawn, where they tripped her as joyously as they did the nuns once they felt comfortable with her, shouting her name for the ball and blocking her brutally at the goal, and she was black and blue and happy when she left them.

She had just been to the monastery for the third time the following week, when Xavier called her. She hadn't heard from him since their Basque dinner in Biarritz, and she assumed that he was busy. He suggested they have lunch at the dower house after the choir mass on Sunday and she accepted with pleasure. He made pasta, a frittata, and a salad, and poured her a glass of wine when they sat down to lunch in his kitchen. He said he liked to cook.

"I'm sorry I haven't called you. I had a busy week." She didn't expect him to call, but it was nice to see him. "I hear you've been volunteering at the monastery." News traveled fast in a tiny village. The woman where Sabrina bought her groceries knew about it too, and had mentioned it after the first time.

"I love being with the children. Which reminds me, the nun in charge of the school told me about your grandmother." He smiled when she said it.

"She was a remarkable woman. She lived to be a hundred

and one. She helped dig the tunnels herself. It was her idea. And incredibly, they never got caught during the war. I think they had some very close calls. My father remembered playing with the other children. She got them all to safety, more than nine hundred of them in six years."

"Are the tunnels still there?" Sabrina was fascinated by the story. Xavier had impressive ancestors. And he was impressive too. He seemed in good spirits while they talked over the lunch he had made.

"They were destroyed after the war. My friends and I tried to find some remnant of them, but we never did. I think that's why my grandmother had them filled in. She didn't want anyone getting trapped or buried down there.

"I got pulled into a crazy project this week," he told her with a gleam in his eye. He seemed happier than he was before. And so was she. The children had cheered her, and spending two days a week at the monastery made her feel useful. She hadn't told her own children about it, but she was enjoying it thoroughly. And Sister Anne was an interesting, intelligent woman. She had been a history teacher before joining the order, and was wise about the world. She wasn't a total innocent. She had been engaged, and her fiancé died of a brain tumor, which had inspired her decision, and she said she was happy with the life she led. Sabrina couldn't see herself making a similar choice, but she respected Sister Anne's. She was shocked to learn that they were the same age, and like most of the nuns, Sister Anne didn't look it. Spared from some of the griefs of the world, they didn't show their age, and always seemed peaceful to Sabrina.

"Tell me about your project," Sabrina encouraged Xavier.

"I got a call from a friend I went to school with, and he wanted my advice. There's an old hotel a few miles up the coast. It closed when the owner died, when we were in our teens, about forty years ago. It was quite luxurious, and fell to rack and ruin. No one ever bought it, apparently it would have been too costly to repair and the bank never sold it. They recently decided to get rid of it, and my school friend wants to buy it, fix it up, and run it as a luxury hotel. It's not a five-star palace like the Hôtel du Palais, but I think if we pumped enough money into it, we could turn it into a very elegant hotel. It's Victorian, and it looks out over the ocean. We could do a spa there. It's a big project, and he wanted to know what I thought and how much it would cost to fix it up. We met with a contractor and some builders for estimates. It would take a lot, but I think we could get the same result for less, doing some of the work ourselves and with locals. It sits on a nice chunk of land and I think everyone has forgotten about it. Someone almost bought it about twenty years ago but backed out. I don't know,

Sabrina. . . . I'm tempted. He wants me to go in as a partner. He would have more money to put into it if he had a partner. I could borrow against the château. I've never done that before. But do I really want to own a hotel, and take on all the headaches of that, and rebuilding it? There's a lot of work to restore what's already there. But the bones are great." His eyes were bright as he spoke of it and he sounded excited. "He wants me as an equal partner, he says he has no imagination, he's an accountant, and he thinks together we could do it, and maybe sell it in a few years, or keep it if it turns out to be profitable. I've been looking for a job as a CEO, I'm not sure I want to be a contractor and a hotel owner." He looked worried, but excited, and she was happy to see it, despite his misgivings.

"Which way are you leaning?" she asked him, and he looked suddenly mischievous.

"My friend thinks we could do it for just over a million euros if we're very careful. It sounds crazy, but it's the first project that has excited me since the start-up went down the tubes. I like the idea of building on something and restoring it to its original beauty. Something you can see and get your hands on, not something abstract that no one understands. There is nothing like brick and mortar. If we do it right, we can't lose. There's no prestige to it, it's nothing like my old job, but it might be fun to do. And I can still go to Paris for interviews if something surfaces. But I'd be busy when I'm here, which I like." She thought that was a good idea too. "Sabrina, would you come and look at it with me? You have fabulous taste."

"I've never remodeled a hotel," she reminded him.

"No, but you said you took your house in Malibu down to the studs when you remodeled it. So you have some idea of what's involved." She was flattered to be asked, and agreed to go with him. He still had the keys the bank had given him, and they went that afternoon after lunch. There was a spring in his step when they walked out to the car and he thanked her for going with him.

"This is fun," she said, smiling. She loved talking to him and hearing about his plans.

When they got to the hotel, she expected to see an old building that had fallen into disrepair. And it definitely needed a great deal of work. But she didn't expect the hotel to be as big or as beautiful as it was. Xavier told her what his vision was, with terraced grounds and beautiful gardens. There was another building where they could rent out space to luxury shops. And an enormous indoor pool in its own Victorian building that hotel guests could use in winter. And space to build an outdoor pool as well. The entire property sat on a cliff overlooking the ocean, and when Xavier looked around, he could see everything he envisioned, and so could Sabrina when he explained it to her. She looked excited too. It was going to be a big project, but both men thought they could keep a rein on it, and achieve a great look for a reasonable price.

"And then we'd have to run it and staff it, but first we have to restore it," he said.

"It's a big project," she said cautiously, and he grinned.

"I know, and it sounds crazy but I love it. It's another gamble but I think this one would be a winner." It was a much smaller project than his global travel service. And for some reason, she thought it would be a winner too. The bug of his enthusiasm was contagious, which was half the battle. If he believed in it enough, he could do it, with the right partner, and he was confident about the one he had. "He'd give me carte blanche with the design aspect, and everything construction and architectural. He's a genius with the finance aspect and making the budget work."

"How long do you think it would take?" That was a factor too.

"Six or seven months if we stay hard on it, and use local builders. They're cheaper and they're here. If we start bringing them in from Paris, it'll kill us, at Paris prices. I'm dying to do it," he admitted to Sabrina. He hardly knew her, but he trusted her judgment. She was a smart, sensible woman.

"Then you should do it. If you love the project, you'll overcome the problems, and find a way." It was practical advice and gave him the courage to make the decision. They talked about it all the way back to Arcangues. He dropped her off at the château and she thanked him for lunch, and the next morning he knocked on her back door, and she opened it, still in her dressing gown. She was having breakfast in the kitchen.

"I'm going to do it," he said in a hoarse voice. He looked like he'd been up all night, wrestling with the decision. He looked stressed but relieved. "I'll take the loan for my share from the château, and pay it back when we make some money."

"Congratulations, I'm excited for you," she said, smiling at him, and invited him in for coffee. He could hardly sit still as he told her his plans, in greater detail than the day before. He'd been making detailed notes all night.

"If we need more money, we can get additional investors. This is going to be the gem of Biarritz," he said, and showed her some drawings he had made. She was happy for him, and proud of him, although she had no right to be. She was as excited as he was, and they went back to look at it again that afternoon. He had already called the bank, where they knew him well, and they were going to lend him the amount he wanted, with the château as collateral. It was an amount he felt sure he could repay if the project was a success.

And before they opened the hotel, there would be marketing and publicity to do. They would have to hire an agency or a team to do it, but there were groups that handled the launch of hotels, and Xavier was sure he could find the right people or do it himself. He turned to Sabrina then.

"Does this mean I'll be a contractor and never a CEO again? Is this some kind of message from the universe to lower my sights? What am I doing here?" He was worried.

"You're having fun, Xavier. That's not a crime. It's allowed. That's the whole idea. You're allowed to have this go right, make some money, and have fun at it. If you trust your partner and think he's the right guy, then why not do something fun? You can still be a CEO later, or anything you want to be, and even create another start-up. Bon Voyage was a great idea. The pandemic killed it. It's open season and this is a clean slate. I have total faith in you to do a beautiful job on this new project."

"Why?" He frowned at her. "You hardly know me."

"I know you better than you think. I've been listening to you, and it sounds like a good project to me too. I don't know anything about remodeling a hotel, or running one, but I have faith that you can figure it out as you go along.

And if you make mistakes, you'll correct them. Maybe doing something different is a better way to get going again."

"I'm going to do it," he said in a voice that was barely audible, but filled with conviction. He left after his cup of coffee and went back to the dower house to make some calls. He wanted to tell his school friend he was in, as equal partners. They had a lot of groundwork to do, and he could hardly wait to get started. He had paid attention to everything Sabrina said.

Sabrina sat in the kitchen thinking about it afterward, and it occurred to her that the beautiful old hotel Xavier wanted to remodel was like her renting the château in Arcangues. It might not be their path forever, but it was the jump start they needed to get a foothold back into life and into the world. And there was nothing wrong with that. Sabrina hoped it would work out for him. From all that he had said to her, during dinner and over lunch, it sounded like he had had a brutal three years and needed a way back to a big corporate job, or a special project of some kind like his start-up, which hadn't worked out. She could sense that he needed confidence, and he admitted that he needed money. Her renting the château was only a stopgap until he got back into the business world again to replace what he'd lost. He'd been humble admitting it to her, and she wondered if it was easier talking to a relative stranger he had no history with. She had confided in him too. They had each found a sympathetic ear, and someone they could relate to. The hallmark of the relationship they were forming with each other was kindness. People had gotten so isolated during the pandemic that neither of them had anyone to talk to. Sabrina was far from home and her children, and Xavier appeared to derive no comfort from his wife, which seemed unfortunate to Sabrina. The relationship he had with Brigitte was entirely the opposite of everything she had shared with Malcolm, which made his absence so much harder, and made it so tempting to reach out to Xavier as a friend. Their respective loneliness, for different reasons, created an unexpected bond. She was happy to encourage him if it helped him. They were each searching for something to hold on to in the aftermath of the storm of the past few years. It made sense to her, and even though they didn't know each other well, their isolation was similar, and she wished him well. She could tell that he was a good person, and he had the same feeling about her. Her turning up to rent the château at the right time was a fortuitous accident for them both. They expected nothing from each other, but were grateful for the comfort they got.

When Sabrina went back to the monastery the next time she volunteered, she got the feeling that the residential quarters for the children were even more crowded than before. She mentioned it in passing to Sister Anne.

"Am I imagining it or are there more kids here?" Sister Anne nodded.

"There was a fire in Bordeaux two days ago, and a convent that housed eighty children burned down. It was one of our largest facilities. They had to ship the children all over France. We took three, and we shouldn't even have done that. We converted a supply closet with three cots. If the authorities check on us, they could shut us down. Fortunately, they never do. Mother Regina has a big heart, she couldn't say no."

The dining hall was noisier than ever, and the games on the lawn more boisterous. The three newcomers were hesitant to join the fun and watched from the sidelines. Sabrina spoke to them in her halting French and they smiled at her. She finally got one of them to come and play while the others watched. Watching the convent burn down, which was the only home they had now, had been traumatic for them. Their life had been one disaster after another, and Sabrina's heart ached for them. For a myriad of different reasons, the children at the monastery had been through so much. She stayed later than usual and helped with baths. She was soaked when she got home. She changed into a warm nightgown and put on a thick robe, scrambled some eggs for herself, and poured a glass of wine. Coco and Lizzie called her that night, and they sounded happy. She had forgotten that it was Valentine's Day, but they remembered. She kept losing track of the days in Arcangues. She thought of Malcolm after they hung up. He always sent her flowers and gave her a piece of jewelry on Valentine's Day, even if something small. He had been unfailingly thoughtful. It was her first Valentine's Day without him.

She was arranging a linen closet the next day, when her cellphone rang, and she was surprised to hear Sister Anne's voice, recognizing it immediately. The nun sounded serious.

"Are you coming in today?" she asked, and Sabrina hesitated. She had a list of things she wanted to do around the house, but none of it was urgent.

"Do you want me to?" Sabrina asked her. She wondered if she had done something wrong the day before, without knowing it.

"Mother Regina asked me to call you. I think she'd like it."

"Of course. If that's all right, I'll come in about an hour." She could finish the linen closet later, it wasn't important.

"See you then," Sister Anne said cheerfully, sounding more like herself.

Sabrina showered and dressed. She was occupying

Xavier's master suite, and he had a powerful shower, which he had admitted he missed. The dower house was very old-fashioned and only had the original bathtubs that had been installed sixty years before in the last update. She loved his suite because his bedroom and the little sitting room next to it looked out over the gardens. The one his wife normally occupied looked out toward a forest and was darker.

She drove to the monastery and knew the children would be eating lunch by then. They'd had choir practice that morning, and Sabrina was sorry she'd missed it. It was an exquisite sound.

She walked up the steps to the Mother Superior's office and found Sister Anne waiting outside the door for her, chatting with the Superior quietly. Sabrina had the feeling that something important was happening.

"Is something wrong?" she asked them both with a feeling of dread that she had offended someone or upset a child. Mother Regina smiled at her.

"Of course not, my dear. I have a question to ask you. It's rather unusual, I'm afraid. Come into my office." Sabrina followed them into a dark wood-paneled room with a crucifix on the wall. The Mother Superior's office was directly behind the chapel, and they could hear one of the nuns practicing on the organ for the Sunday service.

"We've had a call from a sister convent in Saint-Jean-de-Luz, not far from here. They have two children who've been living with a neighbor. The father died in the first wave of Covid four years ago. The children were barely more than infants. And the mother went to look for work in Spain two years ago and was never heard from again. There's a grandmother, but no one has been able to find her. Social Services have been working on it, and the bishop's office. The children can't be adopted until we know about their relatives, and the neighbor has been happy to foster them. She's just been transferred in her job and is moving to London, and she can't take them with her. They're as crowded in Saint-Jean-de-Luz as we are, and we're over capacity now. I can't come up with a single bed for them, and after the fire in Bordeaux, no one has room for them. I don't want to turn them over to the State services. We've never done this before, but you have a houseful of bedrooms at Bonport. Is there any chance you would take them for a few weeks till we figure out something else? I know it's a lot to ask, but I have nowhere else to put them, and I would trust you with them." Both nuns looked at her intently, as Sabrina thought about it. She hadn't expected anything like it, and had thought she was in trouble. She didn't know what to answer. She was no longer set up for a life with children. It hadn't even occurred to her. She loved volunteering at the monastery, but it would be very different having them live with her.

"How old are they?"

Sister Anne answered for the Superior.

"Five and seven. The little boy is five, his sister is seven. The woman who has been taking care of them says they're very well behaved and extremely shy. The boy doesn't remember either parent, but the girl remembers her mother. The grandmother doesn't know they exist, so she's not looking for them. The mother ran away at seventeen, when she found out she was pregnant. Most of our children have complicated stories." Sabrina didn't know what to say at first. "Apparently the woman who has been fostering them was only notified of the move a few days ago. She's been trying to work it out, but she can't. She's going to be living in a single room, and she can't afford childcare. She lives with her mother in Saint-Jean-de-Luz, and her mother has been helping to take care of them. They think the children's mother might be dead or they'd have heard from her by now. They said their mother loves them but isn't reliable. The young woman who has been responsible for them is leaving in two days. And her mother says that caring for them alone is too much for her." Fostering two children was the biggest decision Sabrina had made in a year. She was worried that with their complicated history of abandonment, she might do something wrong for them and make things worse without meaning to, and they were surely going to suffer when the only people they knew as family would disappear from their lives suddenly. She thought of Xavier's grandmother and the children she had rescued. She surely hadn't asked for a psychological evaluation before she saved them, and those children had faced much more traumatic situations. Most of them had never seen their parents again, they had died in the camps. Almost all of those children had been orphans by the end of the war. But these two might already be orphans now and the grandmother might never be found.

"Of course they can go to school here at the monastery with the others. And as soon as we have beds for them we'd take them off your hands. We're trying to keep them together since that will be the only constant they know, each other. I'm sorry to ask it of you. It was the only thing Sister Anne and I could think of. Two of our adolescents will be leaving in a few months, and we'll have bed space then, but we're way over our limit now, and will be then too."

"Can I think about it for a day?" Sabrina asked them. "I just need to run it through my mind. My children will be coming at some point, and I don't know how they would feel about it." She'd been putting off telling them about her volunteer work at the monastery, on the off chance that they'd be jealous or would think she was losing her mind, even more so now if she had two of the children living at the château. She had no idea how they'd react, or even how she felt about it herself, but a part of her wanted to help.

"Of course," Mother Regina answered. "I realize it's a big decision, even for a short time. It's the responsibility for two human beings. That's never a small thing."

"I want to be sure I can give them what they need." She still didn't feel a hundred percent herself since losing Malcolm. It was one thing to run away to a village in France and rent a château, it was way more than that to take in two very young children to live with her.

"Maybe you should discuss it with your children," Sister Anne suggested, and Sabrina slowly shook her head.

"No, it's my decision. These children will only come for a short time. If I feel I can do it for them, I will. I'll let you know in the morning," Sabrina promised and stood up. She had a lot to think about. She wanted some quiet time alone. She was still young enough to have children that age, but her children had been fairly grown up for a long time. Young children were no longer a part of her life, and she wasn't ready for grandchildren. But this would be different. And if she got attached to them, if they stayed long enough, it would break her heart to see them go, and her heart was already broken. This was meant to be a healing time for her, which was why she had come.

She shook the Mother Superior's hand, and promised her a quick response. And Sister Anne walked her to her car.

Sabrina smiled at her. "Well, that was a surprise."

"Mother Regina said you're the only person outside the convent that she would trust with a mission like this, even though we haven't known you for long."

"I love children, especially my own, but those two kids sound like they've been through a lot. I don't want to do anything that wouldn't be good for them."

"That's why Mother Regina thought of you, and I agreed. There's a stipend for food and medical expenses."

"That's not what the decision is about. I just want to be sure I can do it, in the best possible way for them."

"I think you would," Sister Anne said quietly. "I would put their lives in your hands."

The phrase she had said before Sabrina drove away went around and around in Sabrina's head. "I would put their lives in your hands." It was what all of those parents had done with their children and babies during the war with Xavier's grandmother. They had put their children's lives in her hands, without question. She had her answer. She stopped the car and pulled off the road and called the convent. A nun she didn't recognize answered and she asked to speak to Mother Regina. She came on the line quickly.

"Hello, Mother," Sabrina said in a strong clear voice, and the Superior was sure she was about to say no. "I'll do it. Thank you for your faith in me. When should I come to get them?"

"Will tomorrow work for you?"

"That will be perfect. I'll be ready."

"Thank you, my dear," Mother Regina said gratefully. "I truly appreciate it. We'll do anything we can to help you. They say they're very sweet children."

"Thank you for asking me." Sabrina felt breathless.

"Thank you for being a blessing to those two children. God bless you." There were tears in Sabrina's eyes when she put the car into gear again and headed toward the château. She wondered what Malcolm would think of what she was doing, living in a château in the French countryside and bringing two children into the house to stay with her. She wasn't even sure what she thought of it herself. She wondered if this was how Xavier's grandmother had started, with one very simple request to save a child and knowing she couldn't say no.

Chapter 9

Sabrina went to meet Elodie and Luc Martin at the monastery the next day at four o'clock. She had raced around all day getting things ready, and had gone to Biarritz to find a toy store and bought two teddy bears, two balls, a doll, some games, puzzles, and some picture books. She bought food she thought they might like, including several kinds of ice cream and yogurt, and an assortment of things her own children had liked at that age. She had picked a bedroom close to her own with twin beds, thinking they'd be happier in one room. She was shaking when she walked into the monastery to meet them. What if they hated her, or cried all night? Her French was barely adequate to calm them down if they were upset. Elodie looked very brave, with dark hair in braids and huge eyes as she stared at

Sabrina when she walked into the room. Luc was hiding in Sister Anne's skirts. She had explained to them that they were going to stay with a nice lady in a pretty house. Sabrina spent an hour with them, with Sister Anne translating, before she drove them away to Bonport. She wondered if Xavier's grandmother had been as frightened when someone brought her the first child she had hidden and sent to safety across France with forged papers right in front of the German occupying soldiers. This was a far easier mission.

Sabrina carried their small cardboard suitcase into the château herself, and they followed her up to their bedroom, where she had put the toys on a table and their beds. Elodie took the doll immediately and held it close to her. And Luc didn't let go of the bear for the rest of the night. Sabrina played with them for a while, then cooked sausages for dinner with rice and carrots, and ice cream for dessert. They ate most of the sausage and all of the ice cream. They were very quiet as she bathed them in the big bathtub in her bathroom, put them in clean pajamas, and put them to bed. She sang them a song since she couldn't read them a bedtime story. Elodie named her doll Marie, and Luc had named his bear Thomas. Sabrina showed them where her bedroom was, left her door open, and theirs, and left the lights on in the hall. They were very docile, and when she checked on them a little while later they were asleep in one bed, curled up together. She felt like a novice with them, although she had raised three of her own. But conversation with them was limited, and when she held Luc on her lap, she could feel his heart beating next to her own, and realized how frightened they were. Although there was a bathroom with their bedroom, they both wet the bed, and were up at six o'clock in the morning. Sabrina bathed them and dressed them in the clothes they had brought. She realized that she needed to buy them more clothes. But they looked as though they had been well cared for, and they had brought a few toys with them.

She made them Mickey Mouse pancakes for breakfast, which she used to be good at, and they smiled when they saw them and recognized Mickey Mouse. Sister Anne called after breakfast to ask how the first night went, and Sabrina reported on what they'd eaten and that they had wet the bed, which Sister Anne said was to be expected for the first few nights or longer. The children played with the ball in the garden after that. She made them soup and grilled cheese sandwiches for lunch, and the day went by quickly, with a nap and meals, bathtime, playing with their toys, and more playtime outside. And the next day, she took them to Biarritz for a walk on the beach, where they saw other children, and some dogs, and watched the surfers with fascination. She did all the things she would have done for her own children, and had. She bought them both warmer jackets than the ones they had, which weren't equal to the February weather, and the wind coming off the ocean.

When they got back to the château she showed them the horses, and Luc smiled broadly and Maxime gave the children apples and a carrot to feed them. Sabrina was managing to speak to them better than she had feared she would, and Elodie set the table for dinner, while Luc watched, hugging his bear. They had gone upstairs to get some of their toys when there was a knock on the door and Sabrina opened it to Xavier, standing on the back steps with a basket of apples from the orchard. She smiled when she saw him. He followed her back into the kitchen and looked surprised when he saw the table set for three.

"I'm sorry, you're expecting guests," he said, setting the basket of apples down on the kitchen counter and ready to make a quick exit.

"Don't go," she said, happy to see him. "I have houseguests. I'd like you to meet them." He looked even more embarrassed. He was wearing heavy work boots, jeans, and a rough jacket.

"I'm not civilized. I've been at the hotel all afternoon with Pascal, my partner in the great adventure," he said, smiling. Sabrina was wearing an apron over the heavy sweater she had worn to the beach. Her blonde hair was in a haze around her face from the wind, and she hadn't brushed it since. She'd been too busy with the children all afternoon. She put the apples in a bowl, as Elodie and Luc appeared in the kitchen and were surprised to see Xavier as he stared at them. Sabrina introduced them, and he looked at the two children and back at Sabrina, confused. "Where did they come from?"

"The monastery. They ran out of room for two new arrivals, so they're staying with me for a while." His face broke into a slow smile, and he spoke to them in French, as Sabrina reheated the soup she was serving for dinner. There was a chicken in the oven. "Would you like to stay for dinner?" she asked him, and he nodded.

"Yes, I would. Explain this to me. They're staying here with you?" She nodded and checked on the chicken, which was a golden brown and smelled delicious.

"I couldn't say no. I thought of your grandmother. I doubt she ever said no." He was touched by the scene in the kitchen.

"You're an amazing woman." He sat down and chatted with the children and had them laughing in a minute. He told them funny stories, and Elodie was giggling as he gently lifted Luc onto his lap and turned to Sabrina. "I have Victoire's old bicycle in the barn, that she rode at Elodie's age. I'll get it out for you tomorrow. So these are your houseguests? You have delightful friends."

They continued to chat with him in a steady stream of conversation. "What are they saying?" Sabrina asked him, as she carved the chicken and put it on plates for the four of them. It looked delicious, and she poured the soup into bowls. It had come from a can but smelled good too.

"They said that you bought them toys and took them to the beach today. You got them warm jackets and you're very nice. Elodie wanted to know if I live here too. I said that I used to, but you live here now and we're friends." It summed up the situation fairly accurately, as the children took the same places they'd had the night before and continued to chatter with Xavier. They were more talkative than Sabrina had expected, but her conversation was limited in French. "They wanted to know where you come from and if you're English. I said that you're American, from California, and you live here now." The conversation was lively all through dinner, and Xavier translated everything Sabrina wanted to say to them. Luc showed him his teddy bear, and Xavier played silly games with them to entertain them and made them laugh. They seemed much happier than they had before he arrived, and he waited with a glass of wine and built a fire in the living room after dinner, while Sabrina bathed the children and put them to bed, and then came down to relax with Xavier, and a glass of wine for her too.

"How did you ever get yourself into this?" he asked her, still amazed that she had taken in two children that the monastery had no room for.

"I kept thinking of your grandmother and all she did during the war. How complicated can two children be? They're very sweet," she said, and he smiled at her as they sat in the warmth of the fire together, and he put an arm around her and looked at her tenderly.

"You are a remarkable woman, Sabrina Thompson." And then he thought of something. "Are you adopting them?"

"No, the authorities are looking for their grandmother. They've been living with a neighbor for two years, but she had to move away suddenly. Their father died at the beginning of the pandemic, and their mother disappeared two years ago and never came back." Like all of the children at the monastery, they had a story, and the nuns hoped to reunite them with their family, if they had one. "I was afraid to take them in at first. I'd forgotten how easy children that age are. I wish I could talk to them. I've been pointing a lot."

"They seem very happy. They like you, and Elodie says you're very beautiful. I agree with her." For the first time, Sabrina felt more than friendship from him, with his arm around her, but it was so comfortable and warm, she didn't stop him. She wondered if she should have, but it was so cozy being there with him, she didn't want it to stop. And she was relieved to know that the children liked her.

Xavier stayed until after ten o'clock, and had to tear himself away when he left. He kissed her on both cheeks, dangerously close to her mouth, and she didn't stop him. The wine had made her mellower and him braver, and he promised to be back in the morning when he left by the back door. She turned out the lights downstairs, made sure the fire was well contained, and checked on the children on the way to her bedroom. They were asleep in their own beds with a small light she had left on for them. And she thought of Xavier as she undressed and put on her nightgown. It had been a lovely evening for all of them.

Xavier was back the next morning after breakfast with the bicycle he had promised for Elodie, and he taught her to ride it in the driveway. He was patient and kind to the children, and looked warmly at Sabrina, as she and Luc watched the lesson. By the end of the morning, Elodie was wobbling down the driveway on her own, shouting victoriously, as they all applauded. Xavier spent the day with them and drove them back to Biarritz and raced them down the beach. They built a sand castle, and he glanced at Sabrina admiringly from time to time. There were kisses in his eyes that she didn't know how to respond to, and didn't have to. Being with the children made her feel like a young mother again. She had forgotten how good it felt, and it reminded her of Malcolm when their children were small. He had been a wonderful father, teaching them to swim and ride and play tennis, and all the things he shared with them, as Xavier was now.

"I wanted more children," he said, lying on the sand next to Sabrina, as they watched them play on their own for a while. "Brigitte didn't. She was too busy with her practice, and given the state of our marriage, it didn't seem like a good idea to me either after a while. She's a good doctor, but she's not very maternal. I think Victoire went into medicine to please her mother, but she does enjoy it."

They were all covered with sand as they went back to Xavier's car, and he drove them back to the château. He had dinner with them again, and he cooked that time, and they went to the choir mass in the morning. It was a perfect weekend, and Xavier told Sabrina he was going to Paris the next day, for a job interview with a major construction company in need of a CEO. A headhunter had set it up. He didn't think anything would come of it. The interview was on Tuesday. He thanked Sabrina for a wonderful weekend when he left after dinner on Sunday night.

"I'd forgotten how sweet it is to have children around." Elodie had mastered the bike perfectly by then, and Xavier had promised to get Luc a smaller one with training wheels. "You're a wonderful mother. Your children are very lucky. And I'm growing very fond of your two houseguests." And of her, but he didn't say it, and felt he had no right to. She was mourning a husband, and however broken his marriage, he had a wife. But he loved being with Sabrina and the two children. It was so simple and so happy.

He didn't tell her when he'd be back, and she didn't ask him. He had a life in Paris she had no part of. And in reality, she was only his tenant, and reminded herself of that when she was tempted to want more. The relationship they had was already more than she had a right to expect from him. She closed the door gently behind him on Sunday night, and went upstairs to check on the children before she went to bed. It had been an exceptionally lovely weekend, and reminded her of the joys of the past that she missed so much now that her children were grown. It was comforting to have Elodie and Luc in the house. It put balm on the wounds Sabrina had come to Arcangues to heal, and brought comfort to Luc and Elodie as well.

Xavier drove to Paris so he'd have his car with him for his meetings. He thought of Sabrina and the children she was fostering, and how sweet the weekend had been with them. He was in a mellow mood, and had enjoyed the time he spent with them. He had loved it when Victoire was small. He missed her terribly after not seeing her for a year. He hated the time the pandemic had stolen from all of them, the connection with the people one loved. She had promised to come home for Christmas, but it was almost a year away, and his heart ached thinking about it.

When he got to the uncomfortably small apartment that looked like a storage unit in a warehouse, Brigitte wasn't there and he was relieved. He was planning to see her before he left. He didn't keep secrets from her, and wanted to tell her about the hotel. She didn't come home that night, and he assumed she had stayed at the hospital, as she often did, particularly if she had very ill patients.

In the morning, he went to the interview at the construction company in a suit and tie, and squinted as he looked in the mirror. He hardly recognized the man who looked back at him, the man who was a CEO and had had a thousand employees, and had run the company seamlessly for twenty years. He looked the same, only slightly older, but it was odd to see himself in that guise now. He no longer felt like the same man. He knew his confidence was shaken. Even if it didn't show, he could feel it and wondered if others could too. Something was missing, some special ingredient that allowed you to run a company without questioning your abilities, or how others saw you.

He was tense when he went to the meeting, and felt stiff and out of practice at corporate protocols. He didn't really want the job, and knew nothing about the industry. He felt that his presentation was weak and inadequate. It wasn't a match and he sensed that they knew it too. He had had dozens of meetings like it in the last three years. They wasted everyone's time and rattled him. It was all very civil, and they said they would be in touch, but he knew he had missed the bull's-eye by a mile. It never clicked, and he poured himself a glass of red wine when he went back to the apartment. He had sent a text to Brigitte and said he wanted to see her after work. He fell asleep afterward and was still dozing on the couch when she got home at five o'clock.

He opened his eyes when he heard the door close and sat up feeling groggy. Brigitte looked at him with disdain when she saw the empty glass next to him, on the battered coffee table that they had bought in a junk shop for that apartment. All their good furniture was in storage.

"Good morning, Sleeping Beauty," she said in a scathing tone. She knew from the suit, white shirt, and tie that he'd had an interview, and that it probably hadn't gone well if he was drinking in the middle of the day and had slept all afternoon. He looked good, but he wasn't good, and they both knew it. "Bad interview?" she asked coolly.

"It wasn't a match. A construction company. I know nothing about their business." And didn't want to, he didn't add, but it was true.

"Why go then?"

"I'm leaving no stone unturned. You never know." The atmosphere between them depressed them both. Failure was heavy in the air. Not only his start-up, but their marriage. "I wanted to see you, because I'm doing a project in Biarritz. Oddly enough, a construction project on a small scale. A friend of mine from school is restoring a hotel. He got it for next to nothing, sold by the bank. It's been closed for years. I think he's going to make a success of it. I'm going to help him get it off the ground when construction is finished. I've put some of my own money into it, and I wanted you to know. I haven't touched the apartment money, which belongs to both of us."

"What 'own' money? You don't have any money," she said with scorn dripping from every word.

"I took a small loan against Bonport, which I'll pay back when the hotel becomes profitable."

"It sounds like another fantasy," she said, and poured herself the remaining glass of red wine from the bottle he had opened. He had drunk most of it. "Haven't you learned your lesson yet? And now you're taking loans against the château? Is there no limit to your stupidity, Xavier?"

"Isn't it possible that it might be a success? Is that completely inconceivable?" he asked, sounding desperate.

"Yes, it is inconceivable," she said harshly. "You've lost your touch. You can't find a job, and your 'projects' are going to drive us into the poorhouse. We're already there. Why don't you just give up the fantasies, forget being a CEO, and take an ordinary job?"

"As what? A waiter?" he said angrily.

"Why not, if you have to. Swallow your damn pride and get a job like a man." She tore through his guts again, as she always did. He felt eviscerated every time he saw her. "You have five months left to find a job. After that, we sell the château, or I divorce you and get half of it. Either way, you'll have to sell it."

"Thank you for your faith in me," he said. More than angry, he was sad. She battered his soul at every opportunity. Her contempt for him seemed limitless.

"My faith in you ran out with the damn start-up."

"The pandemic killed it, Brigitte, I didn't."

"I don't really care. It died, and you lost all our money."

"Thank you for reminding me, every time I see you."

"I'm reminded every time I walk into this shit apartment. I'd rather stay at the hospital. At least I have a job," she said nastily. She looked tired and haggard, her hair looked dirty, and she didn't care what she wore, since she wore surgical scrubs and her white coat at the hospital, which was the only wardrobe she wanted, among her own kind. "Are you staying in town long?" she asked him. "I can stay at my brother's."

"Don't bother, I'll drive back tonight." Being under the same roof had become untenable. She could no longer even pretend to be civil to him. She smelled blood in the water and went in for the kill every time. He was growing numb to her insults, which were endless and predictable.

"Don't rush. I'm having dinner with my brother." Xavier didn't comment. He went into the tiny bedroom to change and hang up his suit. He put on jeans for the drive back, and she glanced at him when he came back to the living room with his parka, wearing a black sweater. In spite of the hatred and torrent of insults she spewed at him, he still looked good, which annoyed her too. He had never lost his looks. He was a handsome man, there was no denying it. And she hated him for that too. She was two years older, and he looked years younger. He still had dignity and a natural elegance, and her indifference to her looks hadn't served her well. She had been nice-looking once, but no longer. Her limitless store of venom had poisoned her, and it showed on her face.

Xavier put his down jacket on and looked at her. "I just wanted to tell you about the hotel, to be open with you. The apartment money is untouched in the bank." And he was sending her most of Sabrina's rent money every month, so he was still supporting her, and it was a sizable amount. He could manage on very little himself. He wasn't trying to shirk his responsibilities. He never had, and had always been generous with her. He never questioned the money she had spent lavishly on herself, on trips with her girlfriends, five-star hotels, first-class airfare to show off. And she loved expensive restaurants and six-hundred-euro bottles of wine.

"Thanks," she said, and listened to her messages, ignoring him as he slipped out the door and closed it behind him, trying to forget everything she had said. He hoped she was wrong about the hotel, but his worst fear was that she was right. She had shattered his faith in himself for the past three years and made a bad situation infinitely worse. As he got in his car, he suddenly remembered the scene at the beach with Sabrina and Elodie and Luc that weekend. He smiled as he thought of it. Sabrina was the one ray of sunshine in his life, and she didn't even know it. But he did. And for now, that was enough to counteract Brigitte's poison. Goodness was a powerful antidote to evil. He was still smiling as he got on the road to Biarritz, and left Paris and all its pain behind him.

Sabrina had gone to visit Mother Regina that afternoon. She'd had an idea she wanted to share with her, a request. She'd made a little sketch, and had a strip of the colors she wanted to use. Arcangues Blue was prominent among them, and she showed it to the Mother Superior and explained her proposal. Mother Regina smiled at what Sabrina said, and at the sketch and color samples. Sabrina had added a list of her credentials to her proposal, including her fine arts degree from Yale. She wanted to paint a mural at the monastery, if they would allow it. It was her gift to the nuns and the children. She'd noticed a long blank wall on the way to the dining room, where she could fit what she had in mind. It was the perfect size.

"You're a muralist," Mother Regina said, still smiling. "I love the idea." Sabrina had offered two options, one a sketch of a forest, with animals peeking through the trees, the other of Noah's ark, with all the animals in pairs on it. The ark was in Arcangues Blue, which would be the predominant color of the mural. "I see you've got our blue in there. I love it, Sabrina. How long would it take you?"

"A month, maybe two. Six weeks. It would be a fun project and the children can help me with the prep work, and adding some of the colors. I'll do the fine brushwork. It would be my gift to all of you."

"It's a wonderful idea. I accept. How would you describe our blue?" she asked, curious, glancing at the sketches and the color chart. She thought the idea was wonderful, and preferred Noah and the ark. And Sabrina was going to paint the outline of Biarritz in the distance on the shore, as a surprise.

"The color of hope," Sabrina said, smiling at her. It was what she had said to Xavier and liked the description. She could hardly wait to get started. It would be her contribution to the monastery, her gift. The painting would be full of joy and life. It was a big wall and the ark would take up most of it. It was going to be a fun project. She hadn't painted a mural in years, but now she felt ready to paint again. Being in Arcangues had freed her. She had come back to life, and wanted to create again. She was thrilled that Mother Regina was going to let her do it, and she was excited to start. She couldn't wait to tell Xavier that now they each had a new project. Her mural and his hotel. Both were projects that would make people happy. Sabrina couldn't think of a better goal than that.

Chapter 10

After Mother Regina gave her approval, Sabrina went to an art supply store she had noticed in Biarritz and ordered all the colors of paint she would need. Some had to be sent from Paris, and she needed large quantities, particularly for the ark. She was planning to mix the blue herself, to get it just right. She was going over her list of the colors she had ordered when Justin called her from London that night. Elodie and Luc were already in bed. She had shown them a sketch, and explained with gestures that she was going to paint it on the wall and they could help her, and they loved the idea.

She sounded upbeat and cheerful when she answered her cell, and Justin was pleased to hear it. She'd been sounding better lately, ever since she moved into the château several weeks before. He still didn't know about the children. Sabrina wasn't sure how he and his sisters would react.

They chatted for a few minutes, and he said that he and Arabella had both been busy. Sabrina liked the fact that she had met her on her quick visit and could visualize her now. She had made a good impression, as long as they didn't get too serious or move too fast. Justin was still young and had his whole future in front of him, and Arabella had serious career goals too, which pleased Sabrina. She came from a good family, and she wasn't some scheming girl trying to find a husband to support her.

"I called because we've got a free weekend and we need a break from work and school and the dreary weather in London. It's been freezing here. If it's all right with you, we'd like to come for the weekend. I was so swamped when you were here a month ago, I thought we could make up for it with a few days at the château with you. And I'm dying to see it." He knew it had to be pretty fabulous if his mother was so happy there. She had sounded like a different person since she'd moved into the château. Like the old person, with something new added. His sisters had noticed it too, and mentioned it when they talked. And they wanted him to go and check it out. This was the first chance he'd had since she'd moved to Arcangues.

"That would be wonderful!" Sabrina said, ecstatic. She was excited about seeing him and getting to know Arabella better. They had had so little chance to talk when she met her. And Arcangues was the perfect place to relax and spend time together. She couldn't wait to show him around. And she realized that this was the perfect time to mention Elodie and Luc. He would see them anyway when he arrived. "I've done something a little unusual," she said, opening the subject.

"That doesn't surprise me," he said with a smile. "You're selling paintings by your artists on your front lawn?" he teased her.

"Not yet, but that's a terrific idea. I'll have to try it. Kind of a high-end artistic yard sale. Actually, it's something quite different. There's a wonderful monastery here, with an orphanage of sorts run by nuns. The children aren't all orphans. Some still have families who can't take care of them. In any case, they're full to the gills, still with a lot of children who were displaced by Covid for various reasons. They're way beyond capacity, and I'm hosting two of their children at the château. They're very sweet, and it's only for a short time until they free up two beds for them. You'll meet them when you come." She said it as though it was the most normal thing in the world for her to be housing two orphans, and Justin was startled at first.

"Are you adopting them, Mom?" he asked, worried. He wondered if she was going off the deep end since his father's death. She had been so distraught that anything was possible. And now she sounded slightly euphoric, given what she had just told him.

"Of course not. I suppose technically I'm fostering them. They're basically little houseguests and they're very sweet and well behaved, and they go back to the convent every day for school. They just sleep here."

"How old are they?" He hoped it was as simple and straightforward as she said, but he wasn't sure. She was unpredictable sometimes, especially lately, staying in France and renting a château. That was not the pied-à-terre that he knew his father had intended for her, and that he and his sisters had encouraged her to buy. At least she hadn't bought the château. Justin imagined an enormous old drafty castle, although the photographs had looked nice enough. But he wondered if her judgment was clouded now by her grief, if she was taking in orphans at the château.

"They're five and seven," Sabrina said blithely.

"Who takes care of them?" he persisted, trying to get the full picture.

"I do. It's not complicated. Breakfast, dinner, bathtime, and bed." He knew his mother hated to cook so that in itself was strange. They had always had a cook when they were growing up so she didn't have to. And his father didn't like to cook either.

"That sounds like a lot of work. Are you sure you want to get involved in something like that?" And what if she got attached to them, adopted them, and brought them home? What would she do with two very young children? He couldn't imagine it, at her stage in life, at forty-eight without a husband.

"You'll see them when you come. And it's not a lot of work at all. The monastery is searching for their grand-mother, and they'll have beds for them at the monastery long before that." She sounded confident.

"What made you want to volunteer at an orphanage?" he asked. It gave him a deeper insight into how lonely she must be without their father, and how much she missed her own children. It made him sad for her.

"It's nice doing things for other people," she said simply. "It gives purpose and meaning to one's life." She had always been deeply compassionate and charitable, which usually meant giving large donations and writing checks, not fostering orphans in her home. But life as a widow was going to be very different. This was his real view of that, living far from her, in a different city and country, and busy with his own life, which she never complained about, even now, alone. He respected his mother deeply, he just didn't want her to do something crazy, like adopt a bunch of orphans. And she'd barely been there a month, and had two children living with her. "When were you thinking of coming?" she asked him, and after what she'd told him, he thought it had better be sooner rather than later, to make sure she wasn't doing something foolish. He decided not to say anything to his sisters about his concerns. He was sure they'd be upset about the two children staying with her, and he wanted to check it out for himself before he told them. They were likely to get wound up and panic about it.

"What about this weekend?" he asked her. It was only Tuesday so it gave them three days to get organized and for her to prepare, if she had no other plans. But she didn't know anyone there yet, so she wasn't likely to have a social schedule.

"That will be wonderful," she said enthusiastically, and meant it. "I'll be all set and waiting for you." There was a plane from Gatwick to Biarritz, so it wasn't complicated.

They hung up a few minutes later, and Justin sat thinking about it for a minute, wondering what he and Arabella would find. And at her end, Sabrina made some notes of things she wanted to buy that Justin liked to eat.

"We're going to Biarritz this weekend," Justin said to Arabella at dinner that night, and she nodded. He had said he would arrange it. They had an agenda of their own.

"Was she all right with it?" Arabella asked, concerned.

"She was delighted," he reassured her. "She's doing something a little odd, and I'm concerned about it. She's taken in two orphans from a local monastery that runs an orphanage."

"Is she adopting them?" Arabella was surprised, just as he had been.

"I asked her and she said she isn't. She's just helping out the nuns, they're short on bed space."

"That's very sweet of her," she said.

"It is, but it still worries me."

"She must be very lonely without your father," she said. Even more than he had realized. And taking in two orphans to live with her told him just how much lonelier she was than he had ever understood, or could begin to imagine.

Justin and Arabella arrived right on time, at eight o'clock on Friday night after a short flight, and were met by a car and driver Sabrina had arranged through the concierge at the Hôtel du Palais. He had been very efficient at organizing everything. And she had bought all of Justin's favorite foods, and some very nice bottles of wine.

She had picked a very pretty room for Luc and Elodie next to hers. And she had given Justin and Arabella some distance, so they wouldn't hear Elodie and Luc playing in the morning, and the children wouldn't wake them. They were at the château by nine since they had only brought carry-on, and Sabrina was eagerly awaiting them. She came out of the château as soon as she heard the car arrive, and hugged them both. Arabella was wearing jeans and a warm red coat, and Justin was wearing a down jacket and jeans, and carrying a leather backpack. They looked like what they were, affluent, well-cared-for young people with wealthy parents. All of their accessories were of the finest luxury brands they normally wouldn't buy themselves. Sabrina had bought Justin his at Hermès, and he had bought Arabella's at Louis Vuitton.

Justin was impressed by the château as soon as he saw it, and stood admiring it for a minute while they stood outside. It was elegant, and beautifully maintained, surrounded by beautiful gardens. He could see immediately why she loved it. It made perfect sense. There was no madness there, and she could afford it. It was a little bit of a folly to rent a château in France, it wasn't something she "needed," but if it got her out of her depression over losing her husband, Justin could see no harm in it. She had the right to indulge herself, and the money to do so. She wasn't depriving anyone.

As soon as they stepped inside, he understood it even better. The château wasn't small, but the rooms were well proportioned, handsomely decorated, and warm and welcoming. There was just enough patina from being well-worn and not totally perfect to make each room feel livable and inviting. He had seen a similar look in some of the English homes and manor houses Arabella had taken him to in England. It was the hallmark of centuries of aristoc-racy and good breeding. He could see instantly why his mother loved it and was happy there. She had set out a silver tray with some meats and cheeses, a fresh baguette, and a fine bottle of wine, if they were hungry after the flight. She showed them their bedroom and Arabella loved it, with a canopied bed in pale blue brocade worthy of Marie Antoinette. Justin needed no further explanation as to why his mother had rented the château. He would even have understood if she wanted to buy it, although the location was a little remote for someone who lived in Malibu. An apartment in Paris would be easier to get to. But the Château de Bonport had far more charm. It was a special place. She told them some of the history of the château while they shared the food she had set out for them, including the story of Xavier's grandmother rescuing Jewish children and hiding them in the tunnels and passages under the château, which Arabella thought was very exciting.

"So where are the children?" Justin asked her, as he

poured himself a second round of the wine he had opened. "Did they go back to the convent?"

"Not yet. You'll meet them tomorrow, they're asleep." She didn't say anything more about them, and the three of them had a lovely evening in her new surroundings. She had promised to show them the area the next day, and was planning to take them to Biarritz, around the Basque countryside, and to the Château d'Arcangues.

Justin and Arabella met Elodie and Luc the next morning. The children were eating Sabrina's famous Mickey Mouse pancakes when they walked into the kitchen. Justin smiled as soon as he saw the familiar pancakes, and the children politely shook hands, with chocolate sauce on their faces. And Arabella spoke to them in French, since she was fluent, and they became instantly animated while talking to her. In spite of himself, Justin admitted to his mother that they were adorable.

"I was worried when you told me about them," he confessed. "They're hard to resist. What happened to their parents?" Just looking at them tugged at his heartstrings.

"The father died of Covid at the beginning of the pandemic, and their mother went to Spain two years ago to find work. San Sebastian is only about thirty-five miles from here and a fairly big city, and she disappeared. There's been no trace of her, and they haven't been able to locate the children's grandmother yet. As long as there's hope of finding their family, they won't be adopted. And the nuns want to keep them together. There are a lot of stories like theirs now. Most of the time, the church can find a relative somewhere, but not always. They've been staying with a kind neighbor for the last two years, but she moved to England. So I'm a temporary solution, probably only for a few weeks, until two beds open up at the monastery." It all made more sense to Justin now that he could see the children. They were so sweet and well-behaved that he would have understood if she wanted to adopt them, but he didn't say it, and didn't want to encourage her. He thought she needed a free adult life now, not to start all over again with young children at forty-eight.

"Would you like to meet the owner of the château later?" she offered Justin while they ate a breakfast of croissants and coffee and the children went outside to play. "He can tell you more about the history than I can. He lives on the property, if he's here this weekend."

"That might be interesting," Justin said, and Sabrina called Xavier after breakfast. He answered on the first ring. She told him that her son and his girlfriend were there, and she invited him to dinner. He was pleased to be asked, and accepted immediately. She hadn't spoken to him all week. She had seen his car, but he had been meeting with the contractor at the hotel every day once he got back, and hadn't called her. His spirits had been dampened after his encounter with Brigitte. But he was curious about Sabrina's son, and eager to meet him.

Sabrina drove Arabella and Justin all around the area, and they loved it. They walked down the beach at Biarritz, wandered through the lobby of the Hôtel du Palais, and visited the Château d'Arcangues. They found the Basque country beautiful and the history and landmarks interesting. Sabrina had left the children at the convent for the day and picked them up on the way home, and Justin and Arabella played with them before dinner, after which Sabrina gave them a bath and put them to bed. Xavier arrived while she was bathing them, and he chatted with Justin and Arabella until Sabrina came back downstairs. The two men got along well, and Xavier showed Justin some hunting trophies, and told him stories about his ancestors while Sabrina got dinner ready. She had roasted a chicken again and made a big salad, with foie gras for their first course, and Xavier had brought pastry from the local bakery and two bottles of excellent wine from his cellar.

They sat around the fire after dinner, talking, and Xavier asked Justin about his studies and the jobs he was interviewing for in London, and was very impressed by him. He kissed Sabrina on both cheeks when he left, and Justin couldn't wait to talk to Sabrina about him.

"What a great guy, Mom. He really loves it here. He knows everything about its history, and the area." Justin could sense that his mother was in the right place for now. And he could see that the change of scene had done her a world of good. She was still sad about their father, but at the same time she was thriving, and had come alive again in a whole new environment that suited her. He was re-assured, and happy for her. Even the two foster children didn't concern him as much as when he first heard about them, and they seemed to fit in. His mother was good at managing them, and she was realistic about the fact that they would go back to their family one day. It was a good deed, an act of compassion, which was good for her too. It was hard to be sad with the children around. They were a good distraction, and kept her company in an otherwise empty house. And Justin intended to say as much to his sisters.

There was another subject that Justin wanted to discuss with his mother. It was the real purpose of his trip to Biarritz. He didn't want to spoil his weekend with her, so he and Arabella had agreed to leave it until the last day, and there had been so much to see and talk about before that. Justin gave Arabella a meaningful look when the children went outside to play in the garden after breakfast on Sunday, and she nodded agreement. He looked at his mother across the table and dove in.

"Mom, there's something Arabella and I want to tell you," he said, in the body of a man, but to Sabrina, he was still a boy. He was twenty-five and still had a lot to learn about life. He had been protected all his life by devoted parents. Arabella was in fact more mature than he was, and only a year older at twenty-six. There was nowhere to go to hide from the subject, except to tell her what they had come to say. He didn't want to tell her on the phone, and he was sure she would have strong opinions about it. "We're pregnant," he said solemnly, as Sabrina felt her stomach tighten and a viselike grip on her heart. It was precisely what she did not want to hear from him, and had hoped she wouldn't for another ten years, until he was married. She looked him straight in the eye and didn't speak for a moment.

"Do you know what you're going to do about it?" she asked her son. He was shocked by the question.

"We're going to have it," he said. "We're not in any hurry, but we're going to get married at some point, and we want your blessing." From Sabrina's perspective, everything was wrong with his answer. Getting pregnant out of wedlock did not sit well with her. Having a baby now seemed like a mistake. In her opinion he was too young to marry, or to have a baby. And having created a mess that would impact them forever, not being in "any hurry" to marry and clean up the mess did not sound like the appropriate reaction to her. Whatever they did, she thought they had done it all ass-backward. He needed to finish school, graduate, get a good job, be able to support himself, find the right woman, get married, and *then* have a child, in that order. She was willing to concede that Arabella might prove to be the right woman one day, but not yet.

"How are you planning to support yourself and a child?" she asked him directly. She was still supporting him fully financially, since he was still in school. "Can Arabella support the three of you?" she asked innocently. Both the young people shook their heads, and looked appropriately embarrassed. "In my opinion, one has children when one is fully responsible and can afford to support them. No one supported us when your father and I had you. Your father didn't have a big salary, but we lived on it. So what you're asking for is not just my blessing, but you want to know if I'll support the three of you." He had his inheritance from his father, but it was in trust and he was not of age yet to collect it.

"It happened a little faster than we expected," he said awkwardly.

"We haven't told him yet, but I think my father might

help us," Arabella said in a subdued voice. "I just started at Goldman, but the salary is very decent. And I'm hoping my father would buy us an apartment."

"In my opinion neither of you are old enough to get married," Sabrina said unhappily. "If you're old enough to have a child you should be old enough to support yourselves and not be dependent on your parents."

"You were younger than we are, Mom."

"I was, but your father was twenty-seven. He'd been working for five years, and had a proper job. You're in school, you don't have a job lined up, and Arabella would have to support you. And I'm paying rent for both of you right now. You're exactly where you should be at your age, finishing school, starting out, figuring out your path in life. But not married with a baby. You can't support yourselves, let alone a baby." She turned to Arabella, "How are you going to work with a baby? Can you afford to hire a nanny, who would probably require a higher salary than what you make? You both have a bright future ahead of you, possibly together, but you've leapt right into the deep end of the pool, and want to take responsibilities you're not ready for. You can't expect me to be thrilled about that.

"You're even casual about getting married. You're in no hurry. Why not? Is marriage so unimportant to you that it's no big deal, no need to rush? You're having a baby, unemployed and unmarried, you want an apartment from Arabella's father, and you expect everything to magically fall into place, and your parents to continue supporting you." She looked intently at her son then. "This is everything I didn't want for you. The timing is terrible. Fifteen-year-olds make mistakes in the back seat of a car, grown-ups don't. Some do," she conceded, "but it's not the right way to start out. I want so much better for you, Justin. I'm disappointed in both of you," she said, looking from one to the other. "You know better.

"And if you expect me to be thrilled and celebrate, I can't. I think you're starting out on the wrong foot in every possible way on the two most important steps in your life: marriage and parenthood. I can't be happy for you when I see you making a mistake and being irresponsible. The concept may be right, but the timing isn't, and you both know it." They didn't argue with her or disagree. Justin had thought she would be upset about it, but not as upset as she was. He hadn't expected her reaction to be so strong.

Their pleasant weekend ended there. The subject was too huge to be treated lightly, and was the only topic of conversation from then on. She asked them where they intended to live, and they drew a blank there. His student apartment was too small for them and a baby, in fact it was too small for even the two of them. Neither of them could afford to move into the kind of apartment they wanted with the space they would need. Justin couldn't pay rent, but Arabella was expecting her father to come through with a fancy apartment. They were like two children asking a lot of their parents. Too much, in Sabrina's opinion.

"And if he doesn't buy you an apartment? Then what?" Sabrina asked.

"We'll figure it out," Arabella said weakly.

"The time to figure it out is before you get married and have a baby, not after. I suppose I should be grateful that you want to get married at all, but what kind of marriage is this? A shotgun wedding between two kids? Sound marriages are not based on lust and irresponsibility, they are founded on solid ground between two responsible adults, which both of you have just demonstrated that you're not. In fact, you are anything but. And even if your father decides to support the three of you, this isn't the way it should happen." She didn't want to leap in, rescue them, and pay all their bills.

"I'll get a job as soon as I can, Mom," Justin said contritely. "I see your point." He hadn't expected her to be as tough as she was about it, and Sabrina was sorry they had jumped the gun and gotten carried away and pregnant before following all the steps in good order. She would have preferred to see him be more responsible than that and was disappointed to see that he wasn't. Arabella had remained quiet through most of it, letting Justin deal with his mother. She was a quiet, respectful presence. But basically, the impression Sabrina got was that they hoped she would be ecstatic about a baby in their midst, and offer to give them a baby shower, without addressing the important questions. And she didn't think Malcolm would have been happy about it either.

"When are you thinking about getting married, if you do?" she asked them as her final question, and Justin glanced at Arabella and looked vague.

"I don't know, we haven't thought that much about it. Sometime before the baby, I guess, or after. The marriage seems less important to us than the baby," he said honestly, which upset Sabrina too. They were putting the cart before the horse in every possible way, according to her generation's standards, but not theirs, since many people of their generation didn't bother to get married at all now. "The baby is due in September, so I guess sometime next summer, maybe in August, when we're all together for our summer vacation." It was all too casual for Sabrina, and there was a definite chill between mother and son when Justin and Arabella left for the airport on Sunday. Sabrina was angry that he had put himself in this situation, taking on the burdens of marriage before he was responsible enough to do so, a surprise pregnancy, and a baby conceived out of wedlock, with no thought to how they would manage in the future, and the assumption that their respective parents would do it for them. It was everything she didn't want for her son. Their big news on Sunday cast a shadow on the rest of the visit, and there wasn't a damn thing she could do about it. It was Justin's life, and he had no idea of the magnitude of what he was taking on. He was still a boy and taking on the responsibilities of a man. He seemed completely unprepared for marriage or a child. He was still one himself.

Xavier called her to thank her for dinner, after Justin and Arabella had left, and he could hear the simmering anger in her voice, and asked her what was wrong. She decided to be honest with him and not tell him everything was fine, because it wasn't. If they were friends, she needed to be real with him, as he had been so far with her about the failure of his start-up, the money he had lost, and the state of his marriage. They needed to share the good times and the bad, which was real life.

"It's my son, the one you found so charming and intelligent," she said, both angry and discouraged. "He's making a mess of his life on all the important issues." Xavier was surprised to hear it. He had found Justin a very responsible, mature young man with good values, and a lovely girlfriend. Justin had impressed Xavier when they met.

"What's he done?" Things seemed to be going smoothly the night before, but clearly something had gone wrong.

"In a nutshell, Arabella is pregnant. He's still in school, with no job when he graduates. She just started in a good job. They're thrilled about the baby, and intend to have it, and they'll get married 'sometime' in the future, maybe before the baby or after, and 'marriage really isn't important' to them. And they clearly expect her father and me to support them. It's all very vague and completely irresponsible to expect everyone to shoulder their responsibilities, while they stumble along with a baby. My feeling is you don't get married or have children until you're ready to take on the responsibilities yourself." He could hear how upset she was and he didn't blame her. But he also knew that things were different today. Almost all of his daughter's friends who had had children had had them without the benefit of marriage, and given his own experience, he wasn't sure that they were wrong.

"You want them to get married?" he asked her.

"Malcolm and I were very traditional, and I still am. I like things in the proper order. School, job, marriage, children. Not baby before you graduate, no job, and maybe marriage if you feel like it, when you have time. That's a little too modern for me."

"I think that's how it's done these days. I can't think of a single one of Victoire's friends who was married when they got pregnant. They just don't think marriage is as important as we did, or our parents did, and maybe they're not wrong. Look at my life. Brigitte and I barely knew each other when she got pregnant. Our parents put tremendous pressure on us to get married and have the baby. We thought we were doing the right thing for the child. Brigitte should never have married me. I'm not sure she even liked me, or I her, we just had a great time in bed, and she got pregnant. She should have married a doctor like her brother or her father. Those are the only men she respects. She liked the perks and the money of my big job, but I don't think she ever loved me or even liked me. And what benefit is that to a child? Or to anyone? She hates me today, and I don't like her either. She's a bitter, nasty woman. She can't even bring herself to be civil to me. Don't force them to get married, Sabrina. I think that's the worst advice you can give them. They're better off having a child out of wedlock than getting married to someone they don't love."

"That isn't really the problem. They want to get married, they just don't care when. They love each other but they're doing it all out of order. It's so messy, that's not the way I brought up my kids." He smiled. She was a woman with definite ideas, but kids did what they wanted, no matter what their parents thought best, and maybe they were right.

"If they love each other, they'll get it right eventually. Most people figure it out if they're in love. If you think Arabella is the right woman for him, and they love each other, let him do what he wants. You don't want a war with him. You two have a great relationship, don't spoil that for principles. Tell him he has to get a job and support his wife and child. There's no reason why you should have to do that, or her father. But whether they marry or not should be up to them. That's what I think anyway, but you can tell how wise I am by how successful my marriage is." He laughed at himself and she thought about what he'd said. He was right. She and Justin loved each other and she didn't want to risk that. She thought he was making poor decisions, but he had to learn that lesson himself. She couldn't make him live by her values instead of his own.

She thought about it all night, and tossed and turned. She woke up several times during the night. Xavier's words were echoing in her head. She had to be true to herself, but fair to her son as well. She called Justin at seven in the morning in London and he answered his cell. He was braced for another lecture and some harsh words from his mother. He and Arabella had talked about it all the way home, and he realized that she had some good points. His mother was a reasonable woman, she just saw things differently, and was afraid he was making important mistakes. Her criticism came from a good place. He braced himself for more of the same.

"Is something wrong, Mom?" he asked her, worried. It was early for her to call.

"I'm sorry I was hard on you yesterday. I just wish you had done things differently, more in order. But it's your life, and these are your decisions. And even if you make mistakes, you'll figure it out and make corrections along the way. You and Arabella should get married because it's what you want to do, not because I think it's the right thing. You have to support your family, but whether or not you have a baby, when you have the baby, or if you get married is entirely up to you, and I love you whatever you do. You're my baby. And I want the best for you, and for you to be happy. Don't do any of it for me. This is your life, Justin. Try to make the best decisions you can, for you and your child. And whether or not you get married is none of my business." She had come around, faster than Justin had hoped. He was surprised.

"Thanks, Mom. And Arabella and I do want to get married. It's not a big deal to us. But I want her to be my wife. The baby is just more important to us than marriage."

"That's entirely up to you. Do what you both want. I love

you either way, and the baby. I'm not sure I'm ready to be a grandmother, but I'm proud to be your mother and I always will be. You can have ten children out of wedlock if you want. That's entirely up to you." It was a big concession for Sabrina, and he knew it. He didn't think his father would have said the same. She was being very fair.

"Thank you, Mom. We'll let you know what we decide. And we love the château, by the way. It's perfect for you. I hope Xavier sells it to you," he said.

"So do I, but he won't. The château is his first love, and he thinks his role is to preserve it for his family, and maybe he's right. He feels very strongly about it."

"He's a great guy, I'm glad you two are friends. I worry about you," Justin said in a tender voice that touched her deeply.

"I worry about you too, that's all I was trying to say to you yesterday. But you're in charge of your own life. You're old enough to do that now, whether I like your choices or not. I love you. You will always have my blessing."

"I love you too, Mom." They both hung up feeling better, and Sabrina was grateful to Xavier for his good advice about letting Justin make his own decisions and, when necessary, clean up his own mess. He was right. It was a more fatherly point of view.

She texted Xavier after they hung up, and thanked him

for his advice. "You're right. I gave him my blessing whatever he does. He has a right to that as my son." Xavier's response came back quickly.

"You're a good woman, Sabrina. And a good mother. He'll be fine."

She responded with, "Thank you. Do you want to come to dinner tonight?"

He sent his regrets. "I'd love to but I have to go to Paris to get some papers I forgot the other day. Quick trip. Rain check please." And she sent back, "Any time." She liked the relationship they had of total honesty with each other. It kept everything so simple and strengthened their mutual respect. She put the dishes in the dishwasher then, drove Elodie and Luc to school at the convent, and came back to work on the sketches for the mural. She wanted to get started on it soon. And she was glad Justin had come for the weekend to see her life there. And now that she had given him her blessing, she felt lighter and at peace. Xavier was a very wise man. She had preserved her relationship with her son, and accepted that what he did about the baby and marrying Arabella was up to him.

Chapter 11

Xavier decided to fly to Paris to get the papers he needed, in the interest of time. He didn't want to drive fourteen hours. It took too long and was too tiring. He drove to the airport, bought a round-trip ticket to Orly, and flew instead. He'd be back in Biarritz at five o'clock, in time to drop off a copy of the papers to his partner. It was a list of the permits they needed, and when they had to submit the applications for them. He had forgotten the list in his suit jacket the last time he'd been to Paris, and he didn't want to ask Brigitte for it. His new hotel project was none of her business. He had informed her of its existence out of courtesy to her, and she had been nasty about it. All he wanted her to know was that he wasn't investing their communal money in it. He'd done his duty to her. He'd rather fly to

Paris to get the list himself. He could no longer even consider her a friend, she was so hostile to him. And she was his wife.

The plane landed on time at Orly, and he took a cab into the city. He had three hours until his return flight to Biarritz, which gave him enough time to stop for lunch if he wanted to.

He used the code to get into the building, and ran up the stairs to the apartment. He knew Brigitte would be at work then, in the middle of the day, he didn't have to see her, so he didn't warn her he was coming. She would just be unpleasant or ignore his call. He unlocked the door and walked into the apartment. He was wearing jeans and running shoes, and an old battered leather jacket, since he didn't expect to see anyone. He stopped for a minute to glance at the mail and see if there was anything for him, and saw that Brigitte hadn't bothered to send several envelopes that had come for him, and while he was going through them, he heard a moan from the bedroom, a scream, and then a lion's roar. The sounds were frightening and sounded like a wounded animal, and without thinking, he rushed into the bedroom to see what it was, and found himself staring at two bodies intertwined, clearly in full orgasm as the man gave a shout, and a woman's head popped up from the bed and stared at him. It was Brigitte in bed with a man. All Xavier could see of him were his arched back and his buttocks, as Brigitte let out a blood-curdling scream, not of ecstasy but of terror. Xavier stared at her in disbelief. The man turned, sensing danger of some kind, and Xavier recognized the medical director of the hospital, Philippe Prudeau. There was a mad scramble of legs and arms and sheets for a minute, as the medical director stood in all his glory trying to cover himself and Brigitte pulled a sheet around her and leapt out of bed.

"What are you doing here?" she shouted at him.

"It's my apartment," he reminded her. "This is quite a scene." Xavier was shaking, but he didn't show it. He was as shocked as they were, and he looked straight at Brigitte. "So is this what it's all about?" he asked her. "Him?" He pointed vaguely at Philippe without looking at him. "Why didn't you just say so, instead of tearing me to shreds?" Philippe Prudeau was exactly the kind of man Xavier had always said Brigitte needed, another doctor like her. And as the head of the hospital, he had the prestige she wanted. Even if he made less money than Xavier had at the height of his career, he certainly made more than Xavier did now. Philippe was married too, but had had affairs all over the hospital for years. Xavier wondered how long the affair with Brigitte had gone on. Maybe since the early days of the pandemic when she was at the hospital night and day, and slept there for weeks at a time. The same time that the start-up had failed and she'd lost all respect for Xavier, and had been tearing him limb from limb ever since. This certainly explained some of the viciousness, if she felt confident in the affair with Philippe. Xavier doubted he would get divorced for her, but he didn't care.

Philippe was hastily trying to get dressed in the corner, since Xavier was blocking the door to both the living room and the exit, and the bathroom. Brigitte was cowering in the corner, trying to justify what she'd been doing. The tiny bedroom gave none of them room to move freely, and the scene was potentially mortifying, except that when Xavier looked at his wife, he found that he had no pity for her and didn't care what she said. It might as well have been another language.

"How long has this been going on?" he asked both of them and neither answered. Philippe put on his glasses and tried to look respectable, but his shirt was buttoned wrong, and hanging outside his trousers. He normally looked pompous and dignified. He was somewhere in his sixties and not a handsome man, but Brigitte was no beauty either. And she looked genuinely frightened. She had just lost the use of all the threats and leverage she had used on him for three years. Xavier pushed his way past Philippe, who shrank back, thinking Xavier was going to hit him. He was in much better shape, and Xavier reached into the closet, located his suit, and took the list he wanted out of the inside pocket and backed away again.

"For what it's worth, I think the two of you are pathetic and disgusting. I expected better of you," he said to Brigitte, "in exchange for thirty years of hell. I'll let you know what I want to do about it, but I've got a plane to catch," he said. He strode out of the room and left the apartment, as Brigitte and Philippe stared at each other, and Xavier ran quickly down the stairs and out of the building. He filled his lungs with fresh air, hailed a conveniently passing cab and asked to go to Orly. He sat back against the seat, closed his eyes, and replayed the scene that had just happened. It was like an unbelievable movie. It was so sordid, it was more embarrassing in memory even than when it had unfolded . . . the sound of them coming when he had walked in on them, the look on Brigitte's face when she saw him, the hatred still bright in her eyes even then, and more so, and Philippe attempting vainly to regain his dignity. There was no doubt that Xavier was the winner of the ugly scene, in spite of being the cuckolded husband. He wasn't sure yet what he would do about it, but Brigitte had lost all her power in a single instant. The door to his prison cell was wide open now. He just hadn't decided yet what form that would take, and how it would translate to real life. There was no way Brigitte could recover from it and retain a shred of the power she had wielded over him for years, particularly since his fall from grace. But the tumble she had taken now was fatal. Xavier would find his footing again somehow, with the hotel or something else, but Brigitte would never be more than scum in his eyes now, a dishonored and dishonorable woman. He'd been right. She wanted a doctor, and now she had one. But she no longer had Xavier.

He paid the driver, adding a big tip, and wandered into the airport. He bought a cup of coffee at a coffee stand, thought about having a drink, but didn't want one. He wanted to hold on to the moment cold sober and decide what the best plan of action was. If he wanted it, morally he had just won his freedom, but he wanted a clean sweep this time, he just wasn't sure yet what that would be. She had proven herself to be a liar and a cheat and had punished him mercilessly for his losses. What she had lost was Xavier's feelings of remorse for his losses, his compassion for her, his willingness to be generous with her. All bets were off. He wouldn't give her a penny more than he had to. She had lost her bargaining power along with the last shred of his respect.

He didn't bother to eat lunch, he wasn't hungry, and within an hour Brigitte was sending him frantic texts that they needed to talk, that it wasn't what it looked like, which made him laugh out loud. There were seven texts from her and he didn't bother to read them all, the first few were enough. He was going to call his lawyer, but he needed time to absorb what he had seen. It felt like both a victory and a humiliation at the same time. She preferred overweight, balding, unattractive Philippe in bed to Xavier. It was the final blow.

He took his seat and sat staring out the window. He watched as the plane took off, and he saw Paris shrink beneath him. He wasn't going to come back for a while, and he needed to figure out what he was going to do before he contacted Brigitte, and there was his daughter to think about too. But she wasn't a child anymore, and she had grown up in a war zone, so the final chapter wouldn't come as a surprise to her. She was almost thirty years old. There was so much to think about, his head was exploding, and he still felt dazed when they landed. He walked to the garage and got his car, and sat silently in the car for a minute. His head was still aching, but his heart was numb. The tawdry scene at the apartment hadn't touched it. He drove to the hotel then, to meet his partner and give him the list of permits they needed. He was very quiet at the meeting with the contractor, which his partner, Pascal, noticed, and looked at him afterward, concerned.

"Are you okay?" Pascal asked him.

"I'm fine," Xavier said mechanically.

"How was Paris?"

Xavier thought about it, searching for the right word. "Unusual. Interesting."

"That sounds ominous," Pascal said, noticing how calm Xavier was, and almost without affect or expression on his face.

As Xavier left the construction site that the hotel had already become, he felt like someone who had just been told that the war was over and, with all the dead and wounded, casualties and prisoners that had been taken in the course of the war, wasn't sure whether to mourn or celebrate. His marriage had ended on that day, and he felt nothing at all.

Sabrina had been working on her sketches for the mural that morning while the children were in school. She was slowly turning them into templates that would be applied to the wall, with notations for the colors on each one. The phone rang while she was working, and she was tempted not to answer it, but with children in school now, she had to be available, so she answered and was surprised to hear Sister Anne at the other end.

"Are the kids okay?" Sabrina asked. It was a reflex she

hadn't had in years, and Sister Anne smiled when she heard it.

"They're fine. Mother Regina asked me to call you. We have a situation that was referred to us by the bishop's office. It's entirely confidential. We have a ten-year-old girl here in Biarritz. It's an influential family. The parents are separated in a bitter custody battle in a highly publicized divorce. Pending resolution, and given the charges and accusations on both sides, she'd been left with an uncle and aunt, by temporary court order. He's an important political person. The whole situation is a mess. And we've been advised that the uncle is molesting her. She needs to be removed immediately, and no one wants her sent into the public system. The truth is liable to come out, which would be terrible for everyone, most of all the child, with tremendous media attention. They want to quietly remove her. The aunt and uncle and the parents have agreed. We need a neutral place to put her. She's too traumatized for us to have her here. She needs a peaceful family where she can start to recover from what she's been through. Mother Regina asked me to tell you how sorry she is to ask this of you, and you have every right to say no. Is there any chance she can stay with you, even for a few days until this calms down? You're exactly what she needs."

"Will I have press all over us?" Sabrina asked bluntly.

"No one will know where she is. And the details are confidential. I can promise you that."

"Does she have mental issues? Will she hurt Elodie and Luc?" Sabrina asked her.

"We have a psychiatric evaluation on her, establishing the veracity of what we were told. Unfortunately it's all true, and she's surprisingly sound. There is no evidence of aggressive behavior from her. She hardly speaks at the moment. She's uncommunicative, but not violent in any way."

"Then bring her," Sabrina said in a soft voice. "Just make sure you tell me whatever I need to know. I don't need the gory details, I can guess. But anything that would help me to get through to her and make her feel safe."

"I'll bring her to you myself."

"Will she go to school with Elodie and Luc?"

"No. She's not up to it yet."

"I'll keep her home with me."

"We'll send a psychiatrist to talk to her. But what she really needs is normalcy right now. Her name is Geraldine. See you later. And Sabrina . . . thank you, from the bottom of our hearts." Sabrina felt as though she was running a safe house for abandoned and abused children, and suddenly she knew that what she was feeling was what Xavier's grandmother had felt more than eighty years ago. She felt as though she was channeling her. This must have been how it started, first with one, then another . . . then another. . . . It was her way of giving back to the world and maybe that was why Xavier's grandmother had done it, to repay the universe for the blessings she had. To take away their pain. His grandmother had lost her husband and Sabrina had lost Malcolm, and the only way to cure their own pain was to minister to someone else's. She went to prepare a room for Geraldine as she thought about it, and felt distinctly as though someone else had trod this path before and she was following in their footsteps, down a dark underground tunnel toward a light shining up ahead.

Sister Anne brought Geraldine to Sabrina shortly before Luc and Elodie had to be picked up from school. Geraldine was very thin and very pale. She had huge blue eyes and blonde hair. She looked guarded and refused to come into the house at first. She stood outside as though waiting for something, and Sabrina and Sister Anne waited patiently in the hall, and finally she stepped in. Sabrina invited her into the kitchen and asked if she was hungry. She didn't answer, and Sabrina left a plate of cookies and an ice cream bar on the table, and served tea to Sister Anne. They pretended not to notice as the ice cream disappeared. Sabrina smiled at Geraldine from time to time and avoided all physical contact with her. The child was wearing an expensive plaid skirt and a sweater, with navy leather Mary Janes. She was clearly a child from a wealthy home. And she was very polite. She had a suitcase full of pretty clothes, Sister Anne had whispered to Sabrina. And she offered to pick Luc and Elodie up at school, and dropped them off a few minutes later. They looked startled to see Geraldine when they got home. She didn't speak or smile at them, and Sabrina explained that she was visiting for a while. After a short time, since she didn't respond, they ignored her, and went outside to play until it got dark, while Sabrina got dinner ready, and Geraldine watched silently.

Xavier had made good on his promise to Luc and had bought him a bike with training wheels, and the two children rode up and down the driveway, within sight of the kitchen windows, which was the rule. They followed it religiously, and Sabrina glanced out from time to time to make sure they were all right, and she could hear them laughing and squealing and calling to each other. Geraldine could hear it too, and Sabrina spoke to her from time to time, without expecting a response. She watched Sabrina prepare dinner and seemed to relax.

When the children came in, Sabrina sent them upstairs and told them to take Geraldine with them. They signaled to her to come, and she hesitated but went upstairs with them, which impressed Sabrina. It was the children who would reach her more than the adults. It was good to know.

Geraldine ate a normal dinner, and Sabrina let her bathe herself after the others, so as not to provoke any bad memories. She had pretty pink silk pajamas, which she refused to put on and threw in the garbage, and Sabrina gave her a nightgown of Elodie's, as they were almost the same size. She had given her the bedroom next to Luc and Elodie, and Geraldine lay in the bed like a doll, with wide eyes. Sabrina left the lights on and the door open and told her she would be downstairs in the kitchen, and showed her where her bedroom was if she needed her in the night. She nodded, and didn't answer when Sabrina said good night, and she went back downstairs to tidy up the kitchen. Considering what Geraldine had gone through, she had done surprisingly well for her first night with total strangers. The other two children made everything seem normal, and by the time they went to bed, Geraldine seemed comfortable with them. She was still studying Sabrina.

She had just loaded the dishwasher when there was a knock at the back door. It was Xavier. He looked tired and pale and his hair looked windblown and disheveled, and his eyes had the look of pain she had seen the day she met him.

"Bad day?" she asked, handing him a bottle of wine and the opener, and he laughed.

"You know me too well."

"How was Paris?" She had an odd feeling that it had gone badly. And he didn't answer. "Have you eaten? I have sausages."

"I'm not hungry, but thanks." He needed to talk to someone, and she was the only person he could think of that he wanted to talk to.

He drank the wine steadily, and slowly gave her a rough description of what had happened at the apartment. She listened quietly, without comment, watching his eyes and hearing every word he said. The scene he described was mortifying and ugly, but it would have been worse if he loved Brigitte. He said he didn't, and always said he never had. But just being there, standing a few feet away from Brigitte and her lover, must have been as hideous as she imagined and he described.

"It sounds like a scene in a movie," she said, and he smiled.

"It was. I kept feeling like it was happening to someone else, but it was me. I never thought I'd be a party to something like that." And then he laughed. The wine had relaxed him, and Sabrina's attentive listening, her quiet presence near him. He always derived comfort from Sabrina and realized that now. She was the one person he needed that night to help make sense of it and decide what to do now.

"Philippe looked like an idiot. When he was dressed, his shirt was buttoned wrong, his glasses were crooked, his hair was sticking up, and he had put his socks in his pocket. I don't suppose he's serious about her. She always said he's slept with half the hospital, and he's not an attractive guy, but he's the boss. That has tremendous sex appeal," he said. "Women used to hit on me all the time. I didn't take them up on it, but it was nice knowing I could have. It's flattering." She smiled at how honest he was. It was a quality she loved about him. "So what do I do now?" he asked her seriously. "Do I use it as an excuse for a divorce? But then I'll owe her half the château. Do I threaten her, or use it as some kind of leverage? Do I do it the French way, and sweep it under the rug, pretend it never happened, and go on as before, knowing she cheats on me, and maybe has for years, and surely will again. I don't really care. It didn't hurt my heart today. Oddly, I didn't feel anything except embarrassment for them."

"You should probably call your lawyer," she said sensibly, but she felt profoundly sorry for him. It was a hideous situation to be in. He was in the winner's seat because he'd always been honest and honorable with her and she hadn't and it was out in the open now, but it was humiliating anyway.

"I think the poor bastard fully expected me to beat him up

and was shocked that I didn't. I was a perfect gentleman." He smiled sheepishly at Sabrina, and she smiled back. "I had the advantage because I'm not in love with her. If I were, I would have killed him. She handed me proof of who she is with that whole scene. I just don't know how to use it, or on whom. Or do I just put it in a drawer and save it for another day?"

She couldn't give him the answers. They had to come from him, and he knew that too. But he needed to talk to her to help him decide.

"I think you should let it all cool down, not make any decisions now, see how you feel about it in a few weeks, and make a cool-headed decision. It's too fresh right now." It was wise advice and he agreed with her. They walked into the library and sat down, and he looked at her warmly.

"Thank you for listening to me tonight. It went around and around in my head all day and I was starting to feel crazy."

"You're not crazy, you just have to figure out what you want. She definitely handed you a wild card, and a get out of jail free card, if you want it."

"I already feel freer," he admitted. "How was your day?"

"We have a new guest," she answered cautiously, and he looked puzzled. In a soft voice so no one could hear if she was wandering around, she told him about the call from Sister Anne and what she had told her, and Geraldine's subsequent arrival.

"My God, the world is a sick place sometimes. At least that whole disgusting mess today was all created by grown-ups, it didn't involve a child. How badly damaged is she?"

"It's hard to say. I think it's all very recent. She barely speaks, but she followed Luc and Elodie around eventually. I think they will be her road back to normalcy of some kind, more than I will. I'm not sure that she speaks English, I've kept communication simple and mostly non-verbal. She seems to understand me. She's very compliant and not oppositional at all."

"I'm sure you'll be good for her too. You're good for me," he said, looking at her gratefully.

"I had a strange experience today. When they called me about Geraldine, I felt like I was channeling your grand-mother. I felt as though I finally understood how things like that happen. They build one by one. Nine hundred children don't arrive on your doorstep one afternoon. They come one at a time, like Geraldine and Elodie and Luc, and each time you have to make a decision. And all of a sudden it becomes your life and you're on a path, like she was."

"Please don't tell me you're entering religious orders, or opening an orphanage," he pleaded with her, and she laughed.

"No, but when you hear of acts of heroism like your grandmother's, it's so enormous, it's impossible to understand. But it made sense to me today. It happens one by one, drop by drop, child by child, you don't make a decision to be a hero. I'm not a hero for letting three children stay with me, and this isn't a war. But I suddenly could relate to how she got there." He nodded, agreeing with her. He had always idolized his grandmother and been proud of her. And he was proud of Sabrina too, for what she was doing with the children. She was such a good person.

"I think that's how bad things happen too. You let something bad happen once, you let it go by, you don't say anything. And then it keeps happening. And one day you are faced with a mountain of evil, and you must finally make a choice that you've been avoiding. I think that's what happened with me and Brigitte. And now I have to climb that mountain and deal with it. I should have gotten out years ago, or never gotten in."

"That's not always easy to see. You tell yourself it will get better, or that it's not as bad as you think. And you had reasons to stay, for your daughter," Sabrina said gently. Her words were balm on his wounds.

"I think it was laziness and cowardice," he said honestly. "I hid in my work. And now there is nowhere to hide. Just like that bedroom today, there was nowhere to hide from each other. Now I have to face it. Brigitte sent me text messages all day today. I didn't answer her. I don't know what to say."

"You don't have to answer her on her terms or her timing. You can respond when you're ready. You'll know when it's the right time." Sabrina was so reassuring and comforting. She built him up in all the places where Brigitte had torn him down. It was as though she had healing hands, and a single touch repaired him and made him stronger than before. It was why he had been so desperate to talk to her at the end of the day. He needed that healing touch now. He almost envied the children she had taken into her home. They were so lucky to be with her. He wondered if her children appreciated that about her. But he was healing her too, and his advice had stopped her from creating a bigger problem with her son.

He left at nearly midnight, thanking her with a warm hug. He would have liked to kiss her but didn't dare. And too much had happened that day. He still needed to process it before he moved on.

She checked on the children after he left. All three of them were sleeping soundly in their beds. Elodie and Luc hadn't had an accident in their beds since the first night. They were sleeping like angels, angels who knew that they were finally safe. It was what she brought to Xavier too. He felt safe for the first time in his life.

Chapter 12

The only communication Xavier had with Brigitte was one brief email telling her that he considered their marriage on hold for the moment. In suspension, after her blatant infidelity. And that he would advise her when he was prepared to deal with it. It was March by then, and he offered her no date as to when he would be ready to make a decision. She didn't respond, which was fine with him. He consulted a lawyer, who told him that the ball was in his court, which was a good position to be in. Morally, he didn't owe her as much as he would have if she had been a good and faithful wife to him. Xavier had no intention of cheating her out of money he owed her legally. And infidelity was no longer grounds for divorce in France. But he had not decided what to do about their marriage, and

Sabrina didn't ask him. At face value, even to him, or especially to him, the marriage seemed like yet another failure to add to the list, but he also knew it was bigger than that. It was a union which should never have happened, a decision he had made at twenty-six. He had the excuse of youth then, but he didn't now. And he didn't want to make another mistake with how he resolved it. Sometimes the price of doing the honorable thing was just too high. Brigitte had abused him emotionally so severely for so long, and especially the last four years, that he had given up sex for eight or ten years and didn't care. He felt frozen inside, and was finally thawing out and feeling human again.

He was working hard on the remodel of the hotel with Pascal. They had made tremendous progress, and by April, it was beginning to show signs of its original elegance and grandeur. They were going to offer every possible luxury service, and were hiring the most efficient people in France to run the spa. They wanted to offer the best of everything at high prices that seemed worth it. Two important jewelers and Hermès had signed contracts for three of the shops. There would be seven exclusive luxury shops in all, and Xavier and Pascal were choosing carefully among the many contenders. And in April Xavier asked for Sabrina's help with a project she was excited about. He wanted to open an art gallery at the hotel. He had a prime location reserved for it in the main lobby and could even exhibit artwork around the hotel. He wanted to get Sabrina's advice about what artists to show, and to hire a curator and a manager for the gallery. She was thrilled to advise him, and went to several art fairs, looking for new artists. She contacted the artists she represented in L.A. and asked if they were interested in representation in France. Nine of them had responded positively. She selected their work from slides Hallie sent her, and some pieces had already been shipped and were being kept in a locked room at the hotel. Sabrina was excited to help Xavier with it, and the gallery they were building was a beautiful space. She helped Xavier hire a manager and an assistant to run the gallery. She thoroughly enjoyed advising him, and they selected many of the pieces together. A number of the artists were going to come to the opening of the hotel in July.

Xavier had already started a media blitz advertising the hotel. They were offering free rooms to international celebrities for the opening and the months of August and September. Stars being seen around the pool would give it a reputation for an elite clientele. Xavier used all his advertising skills to make it the place everyone would want to come to, on a par with the Ritz in Paris and the Hôtel du Cap/Eden Roc in the south of France. They were using the hotel's original name, the Empress Eugénie. Xavier was working night and day, seven days a week. Pascal was handling everything to do with construction, and Xavier was doing the rest. They were placing newspaper interviews and ads on TV, and in travel magazines. They wanted to make it the most exclusive hotel in France. They were calling it a six-star experience at a five-star hotel. Pascal had chosen his partner well, and three months before the opening, it already had the sweet smell of success.

Xavier hadn't been to Paris since his fateful encounter with Brigitte and her boss, and he didn't miss it. He didn't have time for his own interviews and headhunters now. He was too busy with the hotel.

While Xavier was working as hard as he could on the hotel, Sabrina was working on the mural at the monastery. She assigned teams of the children to help her with basic preparation of the surface, and the mixing of the colors. Only she worked on the creation of the Arcangues Blue, as close in hue as she could get it to the shutters in the village, until they all agreed it was a perfect match. She had enlisted Geraldine to help her when the first supplies arrived, and she became a dedicated little assistant and followed Sabrina's instructions to the letter. At first, with only the gray underbase to apply, many of the children weren't interested, but as the animals began to emerge, and the colors were added, they all begged for a turn to help her, and everyone got a chance. Geraldine remained her chief assistant, and even Luc helped Sabrina draw and paint one of a pair of monkeys sitting on a hippo's back. The enormous brilliant blue ark took several teams to complete.

The work continued through April and became more intense. The unveiling for the village was scheduled for the first of May, on the May Day holiday, with the scent of lily of the valley everywhere. The opening of the hotel was less than three months away, and Xavier had been too busy to keep up on her progress with the mural. She hardly saw him, and he had a look of confidence now when he dropped by to see her, or she met with him at the hotel to show him slides of the artists who were begging to be included at the gallery. He loved what she showed him, and she helped choose the art for the halls of the hotel. It had elegance and grandeur but she had included little pockets of contemporary work too, as surprises, to satisfy everyone's taste in art. The work was by talented artists, some known, some not, just like her gallery in L.A. And the work was pouring in, sent by the artists once they picked it. They had a huge storage space in a Victorian barn, just for the art. It had rapidly outgrown the space they had previously picked.

Sabrina spent Easter finishing the ark in her mural, and

putting the finishing touches on it. After that it was kept covered to be unveiled on the first of May, during the village celebration of May Day. Xavier hadn't seen it finished either. She had done it in a fairly primitive style, so the children's contributions would marry well. And she had added her own talent in fine arts. The animals looked as though they were about to walk off the ark. And Noah had a Rubenesque quality to him, with incredible detail work. She spent hours working on him, as he came to life.

On the day that the mural was to be unveiled, Xavier promised to be there to see it. All of the children were wearing crowns of lily of the valley the nuns had made, and Sabrina stood to one side with Sister Anne and Mother Regina, drinking apple cider. They had been discussing Geraldine's impressive progress, and Sabrina's close attention to her had been part of it. She was teaching her to draw and paint. There was to be a court hearing soon to determine which one of her relatives she was going to live with, and there had been criminal charges filed against her uncle, who had resigned his political post. But Geraldine had told Sabrina that she didn't want to leave her. Sabrina promised to visit her wherever she was sent, and she could come to stay at Bonport whenever she wanted.

As they stood waiting for the unveiling of the mural to begin, Sabrina saw Xavier come through the crowd. He had come from the hotel in his work clothes and apologized as soon as he got to her.

"I didn't want to be late, so I couldn't go home to change. I'm sorry."

"I'm just happy you're here, thank you for coming," she said, smiling. The turnout to see the mural was impressive. Everyone in the village knew about it, but only the nuns and the children had seen it. Barriers and screens had been set up to keep people away, and ever since Easter it had been covered with tarps.

Mother Regina made a little speech about how fortunate they were that a talented artist from America had come to Arcangues and fallen in love with the village, and had created a gift that would stay with them forever. They introduced Sabrina, who had formed a chain with all the children, holding hands in three rows. They all took a bow together, and you could hardly distinguish Sabrina from the children, with her crown of lily of the valley, as Xavier smiled proudly at her. One by one the tarps were unhooked by nuns standing on tall ladders, and the tarps fell to the floor as the ark and the animals came into view bit by bit, until all fifty feet of it was revealed. The Arcangues Blue ark looked almost life-sized, and Noah and the animals looked just as real. It was ten feet high and fifty feet long, an enormous piece of work, with every bit of Sabrina's talent visible, and the children's loving contributions to it. She had had each of the children sign it with her, written under the ark.

There was a gasp in the crowd followed by silence once the full work was revealed, and for a minute, Sabrina was afraid they all hated it. But they were awestruck by what they were seeing. It looked like Noah and his craft were sailing past them. The clouds directly overhead showed the storm, and the sky was blue in the distance, with a rainbow over the island where they were headed, and the faintest outline of the city of Biarritz where their journey would end happily. It was very symbolic.

Mother Regina took charge of the microphone they'd been using and had tears in her eyes when she announced the title of the work by the artist Sabrina Thompson. Her voice trembled with emotion as she said it was called *The Color of Hope,* and then there was thunderous applause from the crowd. Someone played an accordion and the children brought Sabrina a huge bouquet of roses to thank her, and she hugged and kissed them all. Thanks to them, and the three living with her, it had turned into the best year of her life, or the best six months, starting from the worst one.

Xavier was standing mesmerized, admiring the mural, and went up close to it to study it in detail. He could see the additions she had assigned to the children, which enhanced the texture, and some of it was actually a collage of textiles and little pieces of wood. It was a remarkable work that belonged in a museum, and he was still stunned by it when he came to find her to tell her how beautiful it was. It was a serious piece of art with the innocence of childhood woven through it.

"I thought this was just going to be a fun piece for the children. Sabrina, it's magnificent."

"Thank you," she said modestly. "They all contributed something. No one got away from me," she said with a laugh. "And I made each of the nuns do one brushstroke on the ark, so it is a truly collaborative piece of work created by all of us."

"You're a genius," he said softly. "I want you to do one for Bonport, and the hotel!"

"Is that a commission?" she asked him.

"I am begging you." She was pleased that he loved it. He had never realized what a serious project it was until he saw it, and then he couldn't stop looking at it. And in the ensuing days, news teams came to show the mural she'd called *The Color of Hope*. She had videos of the children helping her, which appeared as brief clips on the news. Xavier made Pascal come to see it, and he wanted one for the hotel too. People came in droves from Biarritz and Saint-Jean-de-Luz. Sabrina had never expected it to cause such a fuss. And Justin called her when he saw it on the news in London, as a human interest story. And he said how proud he was of her.

Arabella's pregnancy was progressing nicely, and she was feeling well. She and Justin had picked a date in August for their wedding at the end of the vacation, when both his sisters could be there, and Arabella's parents were coming, and her siblings. They would be ten in all, eleven with Xavier. Sabrina had invited him and he'd accepted. Sabrina hadn't met Arabella's family yet but she had corresponded with her parents and they didn't seem bothered at all that their daughter was five months pregnant and so far unmarried. Sabrina was not as at ease with the idea, but didn't press them about it. She had followed Xavier's advice to let the couple make their own decisions about their lives. Justin had gotten a job in the London office of an American firm, starting in September. He and Arabella were both taking the summer off before the baby. They were meandering toward the altar at their own pace, which unnerved Sabrina but no one else. Coco and Lizzie thought it was great. What they didn't understand was why their mother was fostering three children at the château, but Sabrina didn't discuss it with them. She was happy with what she was doing. It was a sacred mission to her, with Xavier's grandmother as her inspiration and role model.

When she left Arcangues for Lizzie's law school graduation at Columbia in mid-May, she left all three children at the monastery for the week she'd be gone. There was room for them there now, but all three of them were benefiting from the individual attention they were getting from Sabrina. They wanted to stay with her, and she was happy keeping them for as long as they wanted to be there, and the bishop had allowed it. Geraldine and Elodie were going to be the flower girls at Justin and Arabella's wedding, and Luc the ring bearer, so they each had their role to play. Coco was the only bridesmaid and Lizzie the maid of honor. Both of Arabella's sisters would be heavily pregnant by then and had declined to be bridesmaids but were enthusiastic guests. And her brother was the best man. Xavier had promised to be there. Justin and Arabella hadn't invited their friends from London, keeping it a family affair. They were planning a big party in London after the baby was born.

Before she left for Lizzie's graduation, Sabrina completed a project with Hallie in L.A. It was a surprise for her children, one she knew would be meaningful to them. Hallie had taken Malcolm's sailboat, the *Sabrina Fair*, out of dry dock, and was shipping it to the harbor at Ciboure, half an hour from Biarritz, where Xavier had secured a berth. Sabrina knew it would be a tender moment for the children when they saw their father's boat that he had loved so much. She wanted it there for them to use when they came to Arcangues in August for the vacation. They were all good sailors and knew how to sail the *Sabrina Fair*. They had spent happy hours on it with Malcolm.

Xavier and Sabrina had a quiet evening together before she left for Lizzie's graduation from Columbia in May. Lizzie had secured a job at an important New York law firm, and was taking the bar before she came to Arcangues in August.

Sabrina had hardly seen Xavier in the past few months, he was so busy working on the hotel. It looked like it was going to be an enormous success, and it was a huge amount of work. After the graduation, she was going to concentrate on pulling the gallery together for him, and curating the work for the opening show. But she had been busy herself with the mural until then.

"I don't think I was this busy when I was running the agency," he commented to her over dinner. He had been going in so many directions that he was no longer mourning his lack of a job as CEO. The hotel seemed to be giving him as much work and prestige as he had had before. The international press were hounding them for interviews and paying attention to every detail of the opening. They contacted Sabrina about the gallery too, and the artists that would be included in the show. Xavier had done his marketing job well. Everyone was talking about the Empress Eugénie Hotel in Biarritz.

"I think the Empress is going to be the biggest thing that has hit this coast in a while," she said to Xavier at dinner.

"I never thought we'd get this much attention," he said, happily surprised.

"It's all you," she reminded him. "You did it. Pascal could never have done it without you."

"I think we're going to make some very decent money out of it. We spent the afternoon with the accountants last week, going over projections, and we're way ahead on bookings. Our original projections were way below what they look like now." He was back in business, just not in the way he had expected to be. This was turning into one of life's good surprises. They had both had more than enough of the other kind. Xavier wondered if Brigitte was going to go after his partnership in the hotel, although he had gotten involved around the time they separated. He still hadn't taken a position on the divorce and her affair with the hospital medical director. He was too busy to deal with it now, but had promised himself that after the opening he would talk to her about it. He hadn't spoken to her since February, when he walked in on them in the apartment. He'd been told by gossips that the affair was continuing. Philippe was still married, and Brigitte wasn't living with him, but they were still involved. And she had a new apartment Xavier was sure Philippe was paying for that she hadn't told him about. She was pretending to still live in the squalid one.

As planned, Sabrina went to New York in mid-May for Lizzie's graduation, and Coco and Justin both flew in for it. It was a beautiful ceremony and they had an impressive commencement speaker, a senator who challenged them to reach their full potential. Lizzie had so far, and graduated magna cum laude.

Coco stayed for four days with her mother and sister. Justin came alone and only stayed for twenty-four hours to attend the graduation. They all stayed at the Carlyle, as they always did. And Sabrina stayed three days longer than Coco. She and Lizzie shopped and went out to lunch, and walked all over New York. They looked at apartments for Lizzie. She wanted to move from her student apartment, but they didn't see anything she loved. They had lunch at the Mercer Hotel one day in Soho and Lizzie asked her about the children she was fostering, which still irked her, Coco a little less.

"Why, Mom?" her daughter asked her earnestly. "It's the only thing you've done this year that makes no sense to me. You brought up three kids, and everyone is pretty much on track, relatively," she said, referring to her brother, who she also thought was too young to have a baby. "Why would you want to have the burden of three kids who aren't going to stay with you and will end up with somebody else? What's the point of that? Don't you want to be free now, to do whatever you want?"

"I am doing what I want," Sabrina said peacefully to Lizzie. "And no one is ever going to give them the chance I can. Whether it's their own families, if they can find them, foster parents, or adoptive ones, I can do things for them that no one will later. I have the time, and maybe it will make the difference between their making something of themselves later, or believing in themselves, from being loved unconditionally for a few months. How can I not give them that, when it's so easy for me? I have the time, the house, I have the love in my heart," she explained to her, and Lizzie looked mystified.

"For someone else's kids?"

"Why not?" Lizzie wasn't maternal yet, and maybe never would be, and it made no sense to her. "They're not taking anything away from you," Sabrina reassured her, "emotionally or financially. They're getting the surplus I have to give. Your dad is gone, you guys are busy, and they're the little flowers I water with the extra water I've got. And it might make a difference in their lives, without ever changing yours." She made it nonthreatening, but it still sounded crazy to Lizzie. Everything else her mother had done made sense. And Justin said that she was friends with the owner of the château, but that it wasn't a romance and he was married. So there wasn't a man in her life, according to their brother. Lizzie couldn't imagine her mother in love with another man anyway, she'd been too much in love with their father to ever replace him. They all agreed on that.

Sabrina had a nice time with her daughters in New York, but sometimes she marveled at how little they knew her. They knew her as their mother and all she did for them, but they didn't really know her as a whole person. They only saw one part of her. She told Lizzie about Xavier's grandmother during the war and she found that amazing.

Sabrina flew back to Paris and connected to a flight to Biarritz, and went straight to work with Xavier on the gallery at the hotel. She was helping to train the gallery manager and her assistant, who were cataloguing the art and picking pieces for the opening show. Both women had worked for galleries in Paris, but they were young and didn't have as much experience as Sabrina.

She went to London for three days in June for Justin's graduation from the London School of Economics. He and Arabella were getting ready for the baby, and Sabrina was planning their wedding in August. And once she got back to Arcangues after Justin's graduation, she turned her full attention to the opening of the hotel, and Xavier was grateful for her help. No one worked as hard as she did. She was moving at full speed whenever he saw her, which wasn't often enough for him. They were both too busy for their casual brunches and dinners, and he missed them. But he was always happy to see her at the hotel.

Chapter 13

S abrina took time off to spend a quiet day by herself on the anniversary of Malcolm's death in June. She spoke to all three of her children in the morning. They were each marking the date in their own way. Justin and Arabella were decorating the nursery, assembling the crib, and were going to spend the day together. Coco was working, but was going to church in Milan to light a candle. Lizzie was spending it with friends, and was sure their father wouldn't want them to be sad or lonely, which Sabrina believed might have been true. They each had their own interpretation of his wishes for them. Sabrina made the children's favorite pancakes for breakfast, and they had school at the convent. Geraldine was going to school with the others now, she was speaking freely, and appeared to be almost normal, except for occasional nightmares.

After she dropped them off, Sabrina drove to Ciboure to the harbor. Malcolm's boat had arrived, and was in its berth. They had put it in the water a few days before, and she wanted to see it and make sure it had arrived safely. It seemed like the right day to pay the *Sabrina Fair* a visit in her new home. She saw it from the other end of the dock, and it tugged at her heart the minute she did. It was inevitable that she remembered what had happened on that day a year before. The end had been so painful and so wrenching, watching Malcolm slip away hour by hour and knowing there was nothing she could do to stop it. Seeing the sailboat he loved reminded her of all the happy times they had spent on it together. He loved sailing it alone with her. And he loved working on it to keep it beautiful.

It appeared not to have suffered from the trip, and was as beautiful as ever. Sabrina remembered how proud he had been when he bought it. They had sailed from Maine to Florida on it. It seemed odd to see it in France now. It was like a piece of her former life floating there, a reminder of another era that seemed so long ago now, only a year later. But she had filled the last six months well. She still hadn't bought an apartment in Paris, but she was happy in her rented château, even if it wasn't what Malcolm had

had in mind for her. But the château had given her a whole new life.

She wished that she could speak to Malcolm, even one last time, to ask him what he thought she should do now. Should she start her life all over again, or was she meant to be alone? She couldn't hang on their children, and didn't want to. Should she tell them what she thought about their decisions, or stay silent? How had he foreseen the future for her after him? He wanted to retire so they could travel. But then what would they have done? What did he have in mind after that? Did he have a plan, or none at all? And who was she supposed to be without him? He still owned a piece of her heart, and always would. She lay on the deck of the *Sabrina Fair* in the sun and thought about him. Did he want to release her or hold on to her forever? Did she have a right to another life after him? She wasn't sure, and who was she supposed to ask for permission? Their children or herself? She didn't have the answers when she covered the boat again and left the harbor, but she had a strange sense of peace in her heart. She stopped at a little church in Biarritz and lit a candle. And then she drove home to Arcangues. Malcolm's absence still hurt terribly, but it wasn't as sharp anymore. Sometimes it was a dull pain, and at other times she felt peaceful, as she did now. She pulled up in front of the château when she got there, and saw

Xavier drive in behind her. He stopped his car near where she was standing. She seemed quiet to him, and he sensed something different in her.

"Are you okay?" he asked her. She didn't keep secrets from him. He guessed them or found out anyway.

"It's the anniversary today," she said quietly. "It's been a year." His face clouded immediately, and he reached out and touched her hand.

"I'm sorry. Do you want company, or to be alone?" She didn't have a ready answer, but it was comforting being with him.

"Maybe both." She smiled. "Do you want to come for lunch?"

"I'll bring lunch. I'll meet you on the patio in ten minutes." She smiled and walked into the château. Xavier drove to the dower house and met her as promised ten minutes later, with a baguette, foie gras, Brie, and some peaches, in a basket with plates and cutlery and a bottle of champagne. "Maybe we should celebrate him," he said cautiously. "Would he have liked that?" He had brought two crystal flutes with the bottle.

"Probably. He loved to have fun. He was good company." He was a great deal more than that, but a year later, what was left? Which memories were the ones that mattered most? He and Xavier were so different. Xavier was two years older but seemed younger. Malcolm's career had been bigger and more solid. And Xavier's had disintegrated. But Xavier listened to her in ways that Malcolm hadn't, and Xavier cared about what she thought. Malcolm had been a father figure even though he was only five years older. He had been the dominant person in the relationship and she had never questioned it. And she and Xavier were more like partners, or maybe that was only because they were friends.

Xavier spread out their picnic on a table on her patio, and they sat in the sun and talked about the hotel. It was all they did now.

"Will you help me hang the gallery show this weekend?" she asked him. "It really matters how you hang it, an inch can make a huge difference in how you see a painting, and so can what you hang next to it. I want to lay it out and hang it myself."

"I'll help you," he said, smiling at her. "Can we do it at night? I have meetings all day." They were only weeks away now from the launch of the Empress Eugénie. They were opening on the fourteenth of July, on Bastille Day, and they both wanted everything to be perfect. It already was, but he made small improvements constantly. She had a feeling that he was having more fun than he ever had as a CEO, but she didn't say it to him. He and Pascal had gone over budget, but not by much. And they had potential investors begging to invest in the hotel now. It was almost a certainty that it would be profitable. They had done everything right and people were excited about it, both locally and internationally.

Sabrina and Xavier sat quietly in the sun for a while, and then he had to go back to the hotel. She lay alone in the sun and dozed, then picked the children up at school. She stopped in to see her mural while she was there. It was beautiful, and she was proud of it. And *The Color of Hope* seemed like the perfect name for it, with its brilliant Arcangues Blue ark.

She didn't tell the children that it was the anniversary of a sad day, and they had a nice dinner together. Her children called to check on her late in the day, and Xavier sent her a text. "Thinking of you. You are my color of hope. Kisses, X."

Sabrina spent the rest of the week getting ready to curate the opening show. She had some definites, and some maybes, a few yeses that turned into nos, and one no that became a yes. She laid it all out on the floor several times, trying it out, moving it around like a jigsaw puzzle until she thought she knew how the show should look. She left the children at the convent that night, so she could work late.

When she and Xavier met on Friday night to hang it, she had her tool kit with her, and he laughed. He had worn a tool belt around his waist. They were both prepared. She showed him what she had in mind, and he loved it. He suggested one change, a swap of two paintings. She tried it and liked it, and then moved one more painting to another wall and was satisfied. She looked up at him, smiling.

"We're good to go."

"Are you sure? No more changes?" he teased her.

"You can never be sure until they're on the wall."

"Okay, boss." He had total faith in her artistic judgment.

"We'll adjust the lights after it's all up. That changes things too."

"Are all curators this meticulous?" he asked her, as he held a painting against the wall for her and she nodded.

"They should be. I hang all my own shows in L.A., or I used to," she said. "You'll thank me when we sell every piece we hang." He trusted her, as he did in all things. Her judgment and her taste seemed to be infallible. She had never made any enormous mistakes that he knew of, unlike him. But she was delicate about his, and never touched on his mistakes, unlike Brigitte, who hit them with a sledge-hammer and left him bleeding in the road. Sabrina soothed his wounds and touched his scars gently. She was a profoundly kind person.

She had him move several paintings to the left or the right, raise and lower them until his arms and back were aching, and she looked up at him with a smile and told him they were perfect. He came down a ladder after hanging one of the paintings as she was looking up at the lights, and he stopped next to where she was standing and couldn't resist a moment longer. He bent down and kissed her so tenderly his lips felt like silk on hers, and kissing him back seemed like the most natural thing in the world. They kissed for a long time and she didn't want him to stop, and they gently pulled away, and he looked at her, as surprised as she was. Neither of them expected it to happen, and neither of them could stop it once it did.

"I thought we were friends," she said in a husky voice, as they stood looking at each other.

"I thought so too," he said softly. "I was wrong." She shook her head then, and he stood as close to her as he dared and wanted to kiss her again. "You've helped me with so many things in the last six months. I couldn't have gotten through it without you. You gave me the courage to do all this." He pointed to the hotel around him.

"It's all you, Xavier, you did it. I didn't."

"You fueled me, you healed me."

"You did the same for me. I was a mess when I got here in January. You got me through it. But I can't do this," she said sadly.

"Because of Malcolm?" he asked her.

"Because of you. I don't want to interfere with your decision about your marriage. That's not right. It's too messy if I get involved. You need to figure it out for yourself, whether you want that marriage or not." He'd been thinking "not" lately, and was almost sure of it.

"It's not a marriage," he said, but he knew she was right.

"There are three people involved in it now. You don't need four if I'm in it too," she said firmly.

"Can we still be friends while I figure it out?" he asked, worried, and she smiled.

"Of course!" They finished hanging an hour later and didn't kiss again, but he was longing to kiss her and hold her and feel her lips on his. He drove her home, but neither of them could forget the kiss, and what it meant to both of them. She couldn't remember another kiss like it in her entire life. She turned back to look at him as she let herself into the house. He was watching her and looked so sad she wanted to run back and take him in her arms, but she didn't. She walked inside and softly closed the door behind her. He almost cried as he watched her.

The opening of the Empress Eugénie Hotel was a week later, and it was spectacular. Almost every celebrity who'd been invited had come, and the international press was there en masse. Xavier had used all his old connections to get them to come, and hadn't lost his touch. They had a black tie launch for VIPs the night before the public opening. The hotel looked exquisite and the food was exceptional. The décor, the lighting, the service, the suites, the view from the terrace, every detail had been thought of and fine-tuned to perfection. The gardens had been sculpted exquisitely by an army of gardeners, the head of whom had previously worked at Versailles and now lived in Biarritz. The fireworks show at midnight was breathtaking.

Sabrina had worn a simple black strapless dress and looked elegant, beautiful, and professional. She manned the gallery all night to make sure that the new manager and assistant handled it well, and between the three of them, they sold every piece on the walls, and would have to rehang the gallery in record time the day after the opening, so as not to lose customers. Every piece of the well-oiled machinery functioned perfectly, beyond expectation. The reviews were fabulous, and Pascal and Xavier opened a thousand-euro bottle of Bordeaux and drank it together. Their crazy, outlandish, against-all-odds little local venture was the dark horse of the century and won every race hands down.

"Let's do it again," Pascal said to Xavier, and meant it, and Xavier was tempted to try. Either he had found his niche at last, or it had been one lucky shot and he'd be crazy to try again. But he had actually enjoyed it, and Pascal was honest to a fault, trusted him, and let him take it as far as they could. Some reviews said it was the finest hotel in Europe, others said in France. Either way, it was a dream come true for both of them, and Sabrina was so happy for them. Xavier came by the gallery to see Sabrina after his bottle of Bordeaux with Pascal, and he was slightly drunk. He twirled her around the gallery when she told him they were sold out. Everyone wanted a souvenir of the evening, no matter what the price, and all the big spenders had come. There were details that Xavier wanted to adjust and improve, but he was now half owner of one of the finest hotels in the world.

Xavier stayed at the hotel until six A.M., watched the sun come up from the main terrace, and let one of the security men drive him home, where he slept until noon. Then he drove to the airport. He had business to take care of in Paris. And nothing was going to stop him now.

Chapter 14

Xavier didn't have an appointment with Brigitte, and texted her from the airport in Biarritz. He had been promising himself he would do this after the opening, and now the day had come. He was wearing white jeans, a white shirt, a blazer, and navy alligator loafers from Hermès with his dark hair shining in the sun. He looked like the very successful man he had become overnight. He said he'd like to meet with her that afternoon. It was formal and polite. It was Sunday and he knew she didn't work on Sundays and was probably with her odious brother, whom he hoped never to see again. He was prepared to stay at a hotel if he had to, to meet with her. But he wasn't leaving Paris until he saw her. The subject of their meeting had been percolating on the back burner for five months, and was long overdue.

She responded, "What about?" right before the plane took off, and he answered with one word: "Business." He knew she would prick her ears up at that.

She texted back immediately. "The apartment, four o'clock."

And he answered just as quickly. "Lily Wang. Four o'clock." He had no intention of going back to the apartment where he had seen her and her lover having sex. He hadn't been back since, and didn't intend to return to it now. He hadn't written to her since that day either, which had created a misconception between them. Since she didn't hear from him after he texted her that he considered their marriage "suspended until further notice," she assumed that he had tacitly agreed to the affair, which was not the case. In his eyes, the marriage was exactly what he had said, "suspended," on pause. To be decided later. The pause was now officially over, and he was coming back from the grave to negotiate with her. The restaurant he had requested was popular and had a wide outdoor terrace, where she was less likely to make a scene than at the apartment.

He hadn't told anyone he was leaving town, and wondered if anyone from the hotel was looking for him, but if so it had to wait. He had hesitated for long enough to resolve the issues between himself and Brigitte, and he didn't want to wait another day.

He arrived at the appointed terrace ten minutes early and ordered a white wine with ice in it, which came in a big glass and quenched his thirst in the July heat.

Brigitte was ten minutes late, in jeans with holes in them, a wrinkled pink man's shirt, and clogs. It was her weekend doctor wear if she had a patient to see. It was meant to give the impression that she had a weekend life too, which she didn't, unless she had one now with Philippe, but Xavier assumed he was with his wife on weekends. And Brigitte's hair looked like she had cut it with a switchblade and combed it with a fork. She looked no better than she had five months ago, climbing out of bed with her boss.

She arrived at the table and sat down before she said a word to Xavier. She didn't mention the rave reviews of the hotel, which he was certain she would have read, gnashing her teeth and trying to guess how much she could get out of it.

"Why on a Sunday?" she said to him, and ordered a glass of red wine, which seemed heavy on a hot day.

"I'm working tomorrow, and so are you," he said simply.

"I don't see what's so pressing about any 'business' between us. We've waited thirty years to end this pathetic marriage that served no purpose."

"It legitimized our daughter," he reminded her, "to make our parents happy, which meant something to both of us at the time. The mistake was continuing it, which made us both miserable, and is why we're here today. Bluntly put, five months ago, you gave me all the reason I needed to finally end this travesty of a marriage. You have a lover. Our marriage is over, and has been for years. All we need to decide now is how to divide the little money we have left. We have no minor children at home. I have no income. All we have in the bank is what's left of the apartment money. And you have a salary, I don't. You have no claim on me except for a pittance every month, since I have no money. All I have is the château. And if you force me to sell it, our daughter will never forgive you, so you'd be hurting her as much as me. I put the hotel deal together with my own money after I notified you that our marriage was on pause. And as you point out regularly, I'm a pauper now. So other than my good-will and my respect for our long marriage, whether a mistake or not, you're not going to get much from me in a divorce. I want to be fair to you though. So I came to discuss with you what I'm reasonably willing to give you. Are you still with Philippe?"

"He wants to marry me," she said, tilting her chin up, trying to look proud and independent. She didn't. She looked scared. The tables had turned and she knew it.

"Has he filed for divorce?" Xavier asked.

"No. He says he will at the end of the year. He still has one child left at home."

"Do you believe him that he'll file?" he asked her, and she shrugged.

"Sometimes. It's a hard decision," she said, and took a sip of her red wine.

"I know, I wrestled with it too. I can't believe we lasted this long, no thanks to you. And just for the record, I never cheated on you."

She looked at him and frowned. "You must be gay. We haven't had sex in eight or ten years."

"I stopped counting, and I'm not gay. You had me so depressed, I didn't care." He got down to business then. "I'm willing to give you the rest of the money from the apartment sale. There's about eight hundred thousand euros left. The château is Victoire's. And I'll keep the rental money from the château, since you have a salary and I don't. I can't give you monthly support, I need something to live on until the hotel starts paying off, which may take a while. And you can take all of the furnishings from the apartment that we put in storage and whatever is in boxes in the miserable litle apartment we rented. It's a take-it-or-leave-it offer. You've treated me abominably. You should have married a doctor like Philippe. I've said it for years." He hadn't realized how nasty she was when he married her, or predicted how bitter she'd become.

"You were right. The marriage was bearable as long as you had the big job and big salary. After that, it was unlivable," she said bluntly.

"It was always unlivable for me," he said quietly. "You made sure of it. Be careful you don't do the same to Philippe. Men don't take it well when they get castrated every day. I don't wish you any harm, Brigitte. I just want out now. This has gone on for too long. The war is over. I quit."

"I could fight you for the hotel money," she said, narrowing her eyes to look at him malevolently.

"You won't get anything. I notified you in writing that we were separated, and you make more money than I do. I have no income." She looked furious. It was true. "I haven't had a salary in three years, and I lost all our savings on the start-up you hated. Maybe you should be paying me monthly support," he said cheerfully, and she looked like she was going to throw something at him. "It's possible. The breadwinner pays the other person support. You're the breadwinner, I haven't earned a penny in three years."

"But now you have the hotel." Her eyes gleamed with venom and greed. She had an inexhaustible supply of both.

"You won't get a penny of that from any court," he said confidently. "Think about it, Brigitte. If you want, you can fight me for everything. You won't get much, except lawyers' bills, but that's up to you. Eight hundred thousand for the apartment is a damn good settlement. Half of that should go to me, and I'm giving it to you." He left the money on the table then for both their drinks, stood up, and was ready to walk away.

"I hate you," she said through clenched teeth.

"You always did," he said, looking down at her. "You should have been nicer. It might have ended better. We could at least have been friends. You couldn't even do that. You're a miserable person." He had waited years to say it, hoping she'd improve. She never did. He walked away. There was nothing more to say. Even "goodbye" seemed superfluous. The marriage was over when she climbed out of bed with Philippe Prudeau, or long before that. She was getting what she deserved for all the pain she had caused him, and she knew it too. She had no regrets, she had gotten a lot out of the marriage for a long time. Prestige, status, money, a big fancy apartment, nice cars, vacations. And Philippe had set her up in a decent apartment he was paying for. It wasn't fancy like the old one, but it was big and respectable. He said he would move in with her when he got divorced, which she doubted. He was too cheap to pay for a divorce, but he paid for a nice apartment, and she was fine. And he was an important man. She'd been ashamed to live in the apartment she and Xavier had rented after they sold their big one. And the eight hundred thousand euros Xavier was giving her from the sale was a good chunk of money, and Philippe was paying her rent. All she had to do now was make sure he would continue to pay her rent. A threat of what she would tell his wife would probably convince him to let her stay in the apartment even if they didn't stay together. And the sex between them had been good for the last five years. She didn't love him either. But he got her good promotions and raises, which mattered more to her.

Xavier felt dirty after negotiating with Brigitte. But it was worth doing. It would save them both time, and you couldn't squeeze blood from a stone. He was going to make money on his investment in the hotel. It might take a little time to get it, but they had hit the jackpot, and Pascal was an honest man. It wasn't billions like Bon Voyage would have made. But he and Pascal would make several million from the hotel. Xavier could invest it in another business, or a start-up. He had a future again.

He waited at the airport for the next flight to Biarritz.

He got back to the dower house at ten o'clock, hungover from the night before, with a headache from dealing with Brigitte, and tired from the flight. He took off his clothes and got into bed, thinking about what he'd done, and he realized that Sabrina was right. Getting out of his marriage didn't feel like a failure, it felt like a liberation, which was exactly what it was. After thirty years in prison, he was free. And whatever he had to pay Brigitte was well worth it. He felt like a man again.

Xavier woke up early the next morning and watched the sun come up. He felt like a new man as he watched the sky fill with light, and then stood under the shower and thought about the day before. A thirty-year mistake had ended. In retrospect, it was hard to understand why he hadn't done it sooner. Confidence at first that he could fix it, the hope that they weren't as ill-suited as it appeared. Some magical belief that the problems would take care of themselves. Laziness, indifference, cowardice, the complications, humiliation, and expense of a divorce. So he buried himself in his job and told himself it didn't matter that he was married to a woman who didn't love him and hated him at times, and whom he had never loved either. He had wasted his youth with her. But he felt alive again, and suddenly hopeful about life, and that things might turn out right in the end. He felt like he'd been given a second chance at living. It was like returning from the dead.

He sat in the morning sun in his garden, thinking about the future. He thought about his daughter and the explanation he owed her. She wouldn't be surprised, but she would wonder why it had finally broken.

He knew what he wanted to do that morning. He didn't want to wait another hour longer.

Half an hour later, he was standing on the front steps of the château, with an arm full of roses he had cut from the dower house garden. He banged the heavy brass knocker, and Sabrina opened the door with a look of surprise to see him standing there instead of knocking on the back door as he usually did. She was still in her nightgown. She'd been on the way to the kitchen to make breakfast for the children. He set the roses down on the step, took one long stride forward, and kissed her with his arms around her, pulling her close to him. She kissed him back, and then took a step back into the hallway, with his ancestors staring down at them from their portraits. She looked flustered, and upset, as she pushed her hair back from her face.

"I thought we agreed not to do anything to complicate your situation more than it already is," she said. Her heart was pounding from the kiss.

"That's right, we did. But it's not complicated anymore, or it won't be. I uncomplicated it yesterday. I went to see Brigitte. It's over, Sabrina. I should have done it years ago, or never started. The only thing good that ever came of it was our daughter."

Sabrina looked startled. She hadn't expected that, and had resigned herself to his staying married, and nothing between them being possible. She glanced at his left hand, and where his wedding ring had been there was only a deep ridge and a thin tan line.

"I took it off this morning," he said when he saw her look at his hand, as though looking for confirmation that what he said was real, and not her imagination, or a wish or a hope. "I have to warn you though," he said with a smile, "I'm a pauper now. I gave her everything we had left from the sale of the apartment. All I have now is the rent you pay me every month." He and Pascal were going to make a fortune with the hotel, but it would take time for that to provide a steady income stream. For right now, he was managing the way things were.

"I'm not after your money, Xavier," she said softly, and he laughed.

"I never thought you were. And I'm not after yours." What he felt for her wasn't about money. His attraction to her was about the kind of person she was, that he had seen right from the beginning, the bright light that shone from within her, her deep caring about other humans. Her gentle kindness and the hope she gave him. She had reached out to him in the darkness, and led him back from the dark place he had been until he met her. She was an unusual person. She looked deep into his eyes as he stood there. She hadn't expected this to happen, and she didn't know if she was ready or not. He could see that she was frightened and he wanted to reassure her. "It's going to be all right," he said gently. "Nothing is going to happen that we can't handle." She wanted to believe that was true. She had thought that too before Malcolm died, and then her whole world collapsed in an instant. Bad things did happen to good people, and she didn't want anything bad to happen to Xavier. He couldn't promise her it wouldn't. Life didn't work that way. You had to be ready for everything, good and bad. And the way she had kissed him back told him that she was more ready than she thought. It had been thirteen months since Malcolm died. It felt like only yesterday and a lifetime ago, and she didn't know if she was meant to move on, or live forever in the shadow of his memory. Xavier thought she deserved more than that, they both did. And if Malcolm had loved her as she said, Xavier was sure that he would have wanted more for her than living in his memory and seeing their children once in a while when they had time.

She was putting the roses in a vase and Xavier was watching her with love in his eyes, when the children came running into the kitchen, laughing and talking a mile a minute. She said that Xavier had come to have breakfast with them.

"Will you show me how to ride my bike if we take the

training wheels off?" Luc asked him with his big blue eyes and missing two front teeth, which had recently fallen out. "I want to ride like Elodie and Geraldine. She's my sister now too," Luc announced, and Sabrina couldn't imagine her life without them now.

"You have to wait until you're a little bigger," Xavier said, and tied his shoelaces for him, and Sabrina hastily made everyone's favorite pancakes, and promptly burned one. She was distracted thinking of Xavier's news and their kiss in the doorway. Life was moving so quickly, she could hardly keep up with what was happening.

The children wanted to swim in the pool after breakfast but Sabrina said it was too early, and sent them out to play ball in the garden, so she and Xavier could talk. She smiled shyly at him after they went outside. They talked about the hotel and how well the opening had gone. She hadn't seen him since he had gone to see Brigitte.

"I have to rehang the gallery," she said, avoiding more important subjects. "I'll have Hallie send me more work by my L.A. artists this week too. They'll be thrilled that everything sold." She'd been running her gallery from a distance for the past six months, and she knew she'd have to go back one of these days. But Hallie was doing fine without her, bringing in new work, meeting new artists, staying in touch with their existing artists, and running their shows. Sabrina had a life six thousand miles away, but nothing she wanted to go back to, and a house standing empty in Malibu. She had rented the château for a year, and had no idea what to do or where to go after that. She was happy in Arcangues, but it wasn't home. She felt like a ship without an anchor now. Xavier pulled her gently into his arms then and kissed her again, and when he did, she forgot everything but him for a minute. Everything in her life there was meant to be temporary, the children, the château, Xavier, but more and more it felt like home. She didn't know if it was an illusion or real. And what if it didn't last?

Xavier took the day off and they all went to the beach, built sand castles again, looked for seashells, waded in the ocean, and went out for ice cream afterward.

And on the way back, she said she had a surprise for them, and she had Xavier drive them to the harbor in Ciboure, and she showed them the *Sabrina Fair*. They uncovered it, and the children climbed all over it and went below decks to the two cabins. Xavier was in awe of how beautiful the boat was, and how impeccably maintained. He could tell how much Malcolm must have loved the boat by the perfect condition it was in. Sabrina could almost sense Malcolm with them, as they sat on the sailboat he had loved. She felt as though she was presenting him her new life, and Xavier felt it too.

"It sounds self-serving," he said to her quietly while the children were busy exploring the boat, "but he must have wanted you to be happy afterward. He took as good care of you as he did this boat. You and your children are his legacy. You have to let the wind fill your sails and move forward again." She could already feel it happening, and she promised to take the children out on the boat soon. And then they went home to the château, and Xavier cooked hamburgers and hot dogs on the American barbecue Hallie had sent her. The children had had a full day and were exhausted by the time they went to bed. Xavier and Sabrina sat side by side in the lounge chairs on the patio and watched the falling stars that night. It felt like a perfect life when he kissed her, and she wanted to believe it was forever. And now that he had dealt with Brigitte, there was nothing to stop them. She could feel the wind fill their sails and carry them forward. It was a perfect beginning, and had been a perfect day.

After their day at the beach, Sabrina went to the hotel and picked new work for the gallery from the extra pieces Hallie had sent, and local work that had been sent by the French artists they were representing. They had enough to rehang a creditable show. The women at the gallery helped her hang it, and they used one of the maintenance men from the hotel staff to help them and adjust the lights. It looked beautiful when it was up. Xavier came by to see how it looked, and liked it even better than the first show. He was on his way to a meeting with Pascal.

"You did a fantastic job, again. . . ." he told Sabrina, with a quick kiss and a tender look. They both remembered the night they had hung the first show together, only weeks ago, and the first time he had kissed her. Things had moved quickly since then. Neither of them knew what the future would bring, but the present was very sweet.

He bought two of the paintings himself. They were beautiful ocean scenes, one with a sailboat in the distance coming out of the mist. It reminded them both of the *Sabrina Fair*. He wanted the paintings for the dower house. And he chose a third painting he wanted for his bedroom at the château that Sabrina had found in the stacks of paintings they hadn't hung.

"You're becoming my best customer," Sabrina teased him.

"When are you going to paint a mural for me at the château?" he asked her. He was still in love with the one she had done of Noah's ark, with the children's help. People were coming to the monastery especially to see it, and a documentary filmmaker wanted to do a film about Sabrina, which she had graciously declined. She didn't like the spotlight on her, but she loved discreetly watching people coming to see the mural and discovering all the little subtle details, if they studied it long enough. The mural appeared simple at first, but it was filled with symbolism and hidden treasures.

"What would you want in a mural at Bonport?" she asked.

"You running through the forest," he said whimsically, and then had to go to his meeting with Pascal.

Xavier was surprised when he got to Pascal's office, which had a magnificent ocean view. Pascal had folders of three hotels for sale, one not far away in Saint-Jean-de-Luz, another in Bordeaux, and one in Corsica. They were all foreclosures, and being sold for very little money, but none were as beautiful as the Empress Eugénie. Pascal wanted to use the same formula they had in Biarritz, and Xavier thought they shouldn't rush it, they should learn more from their success and wait to find the right one. Pascal was so excited, he couldn't wait to do another hotel, but Xavier was more cautious. They were a good balance for each other. And he told Sabrina about it that night when he came by after the children were in bed. He loved sitting with her and talking at the end of the day. It was a closeness he had never had with Brigitte and cherished.

"Do you suppose that's my path now?" he asked her. "Building luxury hotels. I had fun doing it, but I didn't expect to make a career of it." The Empress Eugénie Hotel

Danielle Steel

was becoming a legendary success. It was the simple, unexpected gift Sabrina had told him could happen. The timing and the blending of talents and experience had been just right. Pascal knew the brick-and-mortar side intimately, and Xavier brought all his publicity and marketing skills to the project with brilliant results. Sabrina loved seeing him happy. She remembered how down he had been six months before, when she arrived, and so was she. It was a whole different world now six months later, in record time. It proved what she believed, that you never knew when good things were going to happen. Success might be just around the corner, not disaster. It was a philosophy she lived by, despite what had happened to Malcolm, which had shaken her to her foundation. She wasn't fully recovered yet, but she was better, and Xavier and the three children from the monastery were a big part of it.

She was excited about her own children coming in August, and could hardly wait. She kept making lists of things she wanted to do with them and show them. She wasn't sure how to explain Xavier now. She had been mentioning him all year and said he was a friend, which was true then. But things were slowly slipping across that line now, and it was obvious that he was in love with her, and she was falling hard for him too. She didn't want her children to think she had lied to them, but things had

270

changed, and were moving quickly. Burgeoning love was hard to hide and she didn't want to. Sister Anne was suspecting something too. She didn't ask her directly, but she smiled whenever Xavier's name came up, and Sabrina pretended not to notice.

Sabrina was happy that Xavier had already met Justin, so at least the two men would be comfortable with each other. And on the last weekend of their stay, Justin and Arabella were getting married. Her parents and siblings were coming a day or two before. They were finally making it to the altar, a month before the baby. They had moved into a new apartment which, as predicted, Arabella's father had bought for them as a wedding gift, which Sabrina didn't approve of. She had bought the furniture for the nursery as a baby gift. But she still expected her son to support his wife and child, and he was well aware of her feelings on the subject. He had started his new job, but his starting salary wouldn't take them far. And he was still too young to collect his inheritance according to the conditions his father had set. Malcolm hadn't expected him to marry and to have a wife and child to support so young and so soon after he wrote his will.

And Coco had fallen in love with a young Italian. He was a fashion photographer's assistant, fatally handsome, and she was having her first big romance. Lizzie was dating one of the lawyers at her firm, which was frowned on but not forbidden, and taking risks of her own. They were all busy leading their lives, and making their own decisions, for better or worse. Xavier had reported that Victoire was getting seriously involved with a young Dutch doctor she worked with in Zimbabwe. Sabrina was philosophical about it. They were all moving forward on the tides of life. Sabrina had no idea how her daughters would react to Xavier, or even Justin, when he realized that they were in love. She wasn't going to hide it from them, but she wasn't going to announce it either. She had a right to her own life, just as they did, but she was well aware that they might not see it that way. They considered her their property, to serve their needs, and they expected her to have Malcolm's mark on her forever, and to live in his memory, to remain his wife even once he was gone. She didn't know if they would give Xavier a hard time, and neither did he. He was half expecting them to object to him, or even try to force their mother to give him up, which worried him. Children could be formidable, selfish, and merciless at times. He just hoped that Sabrina would be strong enough to resist them, if they were opposed to the relationship. Anything was possible. Sabrina was braced for whatever objections they might present, determined not to let them sway her.

Shortly before they arrived, Hallie called her with a

surprise offer. A family from Dallas wanted to rent her Malibu house for a year, which brought up the question of whether or when she was coming back. Sabrina had no idea and said she'd have to think about it. Xavier felt that they were on shifting sands sometimes, with a lot of people and factors with the ability to influence her life more than he could. All he could do was hope their budding romance would survive. Sabrina felt that tucked away in tiny Arcangues, they were safe from the storms that would come. Xavier hoped she was right.

Chapter 15

There was safety in numbers, and all three of Sabrina's children arrived on the same day. It was allegedly a coincidence, but she wasn't so sure. Coco and Lizzie spoke to each other almost every day, and were very close, and one or the other was in regular contact with Justin, especially if they were worried about something. They counted on him as the oldest and the only son to weigh heavily with their mother. There were only three years between them from oldest to youngest, and sometimes they felt more like triplets, or a three-headed monster, as she called them when they ganged up on her, or even disagreed with her. It was too much to hope for that there would be no controversial issues during their two-week stay. And as much as she was looking forward to spending two weeks with them, Sabrina was also dreading the problems she might have to confront, and in-laws she didn't know. Arabella's parents seemed to be very nice and polite, but houseguests were always a challenge, particularly if the houseguests were in-laws and the parents of the bride. Arabella was a bright, easygoing, no-nonsense girl, which Sabrina liked about her. She hated hysterics and drama queens, but however reasonable Arabella was, that didn't mean her parents were. Sabrina was nervous about meeting them and having them stay with her at the château.

By the night before they were all arriving, Sabrina was tense, as she shared a last civilized glass of wine with Xavier. He was assuring her it would be fine, without being totally convinced of it himself. But he felt it his duty to reassure her. He didn't know her children and how they could get on tangents or if they whipped each other up, and none of them knew Arabella's parents, who were the total unknown element in the crowd. Her mother had already emailed to ask for separate bedrooms because her husband snored. Sabrina didn't mind, she had plenty of rooms at the château.

Lizzie was the first to arrive, on a flight from New York. She was exuberant and ecstatic to see her mother, but with Lizzie, excessive enthusiasm usually thinly concealed an agenda of some kind.

She was warm and affectionate with her mother when

she arrived, exclaimed over the beauty of her bedroom, and completely ignored the three children who lived there, as though they were invisible. They had made her welcome cards and taped them to her door, and Lizzie breezed past the cards without noticing them, or the artists who had drawn them and put them there. The children looked shocked and disappointed when she ignored them and seemed possessive with her mother. It annoyed Sabrina that Lizzie felt a need to compete with a five-, a seven-, and a ten-year-old. Sabrina made a point of including her foster children in any activity and conversation, which annoyed Lizzie even more than the fact that clearly her mother had a certain loyalty to them. For all the eight months that her mother had spent in France so far, Lizzie could never understand why her mother had involved herself to that degree with three local children. And without putting words to them, she made her feelings known. Her message to her mother was clear. She didn't approve of the foster children, and had no intention of interacting with them, to the point of being rude. It was perfectly obvious to Sabrina that Lizzie was jealous of them, absurd as that seemed to her.

Coco's flight from Milan was a short hop, and she timed it so she landed within an hour of Lizzie's flight from New York. With an entirely different disposition, she arrived with candy and little gifts for the children, which they loved and which touched Sabrina. Elodie, Luc, and Geraldine adopted her immediately, hung out in her bedroom, and watched her unpack. Geraldine stared with wonder at all of Coco's trendy clothes. As soon as Lizzie entered the room, she asked the children to leave, and Coco whispered to them that they could come back later. They giggled as they left, and their verdict was unanimous: Coco was the nicest and Lizzie not so much.

Justin and Arabella showed up two hours later by train, which Arabella's doctor preferred to flying if she insisted on traveling at eight months pregnant. And while she was unpacking and settling in, Justin went to check in with his sisters, and inevitably, they closed the door to gossip, while Lizzie went on a rant that it was completely weird that their mother had "those children" living there. Was she trying to look young and pretend they were hers? Coco was always more generous in her assessment of their mother and said that she had a charitable nature, and was trying to help them.

"To do what? Ruin our vacation?" Lizzie said, steaming. "They're like little ferrets sneaking around corners, staring at us."

It was definitely the identified bête noire of the vacation at the outset, Lizzie vs. the kids. Coco also thought the château was gorgeous. Lizzie wasn't so sure about that either. She thought it looked threadbare and battle-weary. She was clearly resentful of her mother's new life. Coco wasn't. Justin liked the château a lot, and the owner, whom his sisters hadn't met yet.

Sabrina could sense from the atmosphere that something was up when she served iced tea and lemonade and cookies on the terrace. The children joined them and drank several glasses of lemonade and ate some of the cookies, while Lizzie rolled her eyes and begrudged them every crumb, and Sabrina offered them the plate of cookies again to make sure they got what they wanted. The atmosphere didn't improve by dinnertime, and Sabrina sat the children as far away as she could from Lizzie, who criticized them loudly at the dinner table, and said you could tell they'd grown up in an orphanage. Sabrina stepped in immediately in their defense.

"In the first place, Lizzie, it's a monastery, not an orphanage. Their placement there is recent, and temporary. They've all grown up in nice homes, just as nice as yours and ours. And they've been here at the château with me for six months, so maybe you don't approve of my manners either."

"I just want to be sure they know the rules," Lizzie said piously, in full passive-aggressive mode.

"Ahh, the rules," Sabrina said, fully annoyed by then. "In

that case, please get your elbows off the table. And the rules, then, that you want to make them aware of are that it's okay to be rude and nasty if you're bigger, stronger, taller, or more of a bully than the person you are talking to. Well, now we are clear on that. And now, Lizzie, you can work on being more pleasant to our guests." Lizzie was silent and steaming after that. It was obvious to her that her mother's loyalties were to the intruders, not her family.

By breakfast the next morning, Lizzie's attitude had not improved and she was so harsh she made Geraldine cry, which made Sabrina furious, and she had a showdown with Lizzie after breakfast.

"This has to stop." She put her foot down. "These are children, you're all adults. These three children are here because I want them to be. It's not an accident, no one forced them on me. I volunteered. They're children who have suffered and are still suffering, either from Covid-related situations or abuse within their families, and I have chosen to have them here, purely out of compassion to see if I could help them. You have *no* right to bully and terrorize them because you're jealous of a bunch of children. You have tremendous advantages in life, all of you, all of us, and you need to stop punishing them for being here. They've already been punished enough before you got here. I'm ashamed of you for behaving this way," she said directly to Lizzie, who stormed out of the room.

That night, Xavier came to dinner and met the girls for the first time. Lizzie was chilly with him, and Coco ignored him. It was obvious that they both had a problem with him.

"You said she didn't have a boyfriend, and he's married. He mentioned his wife." Coco accused Justin of misreporting the situation. "Are you fucking joking? Of course he's her boyfriend, they can't keep their hands off each other. That's why she's been here for seven months."

Justin said he hadn't noticed their hands on each other when he had met him six months ago, and he was a nice guy, and he thought he might be separated. Justin's sisters didn't agree with him, and another battle ensued as soon as Xavier left. The atmosphere toward him had been hostile, and he removed himself almost as soon as dinner was over. He didn't want to upset Sabrina, or her family.

They finally had a big blowout that covered everything— sleep, rooms, Justin, the kids, life—in a family meeting that Sabrina ran with an iron hand, while Lizzie tried to match her. The basis of it, Sabrina realized later, was fear, with a dash of jealousy thrown in. Their concerns were mostly childish. Was she going to adopt the three children, and why were they there? Why was she fostering children at all? The concerns about Xavier were similar. Who was he?

What was he? Was she dating him or in love with him, or both? Did he live with her when they weren't around? Was he after money? Had she done a criminal check on him, and was she going to marry him? Was he married or not? Was she going to buy the château? Was she planning to stay in France, and if so, for how long, and when was she coming home?

Sabrina made a list of their questions, and answered them one by one, starting with the last one.

"In the first place, not one of you is living in L.A. You're all over the map now. None of you intend to move back to L.A. ever, so what difference does it make where I am, or when I go back to L.A.?" In essence they wanted her in a box on a shelf in order to satisfy their childish insecurity. They didn't want to be with her or live near her, but they wanted her at a familiar address, not on the loose somewhere, having fun. Fun didn't need to be part of her life, that was their job. Her job was to be where she always had been and not to move from that spot, or do something unpredictable that they couldn't control. Their message was very clear. And a man in her life was a sign of extreme danger to them, and unpredictability on her part. The underlying deeply buried fear with some of their other complaints boiled down to "Who do you love more? Them or us?" It applied to Xavier as well as the three foster children.

In fact, none of the Thompson children had been displaced or replaced, which was their real concern. And Xavier was the biggest threat of all, so they were nasty to him, hoping to chase him away. Their encouraging her to get an apartment in France was a fraud. They envisioned her going there twice a year, if that, for a break, and staying for two to five days. They did not expect her to rent a château and get comfortable. Comfort was not part of the plan, unless it was their comfort instead of hers. It was like talking to a bunch of five-year-olds.

Justin was the least strident voice in the group. He expressed concern about Xavier, but he had liked him initially and thought he was probably okay. He wasn't as upset as his sisters, but he was about to have a wife and was expecting a baby, and wasn't as close to their mother as the girls were. It was really all about jealousy, and adults behaving like children. Sabrina was annoyed more than anything about their comments. They assumed no brain on her part, no judgment, no freedom, and no right to have a life. If she followed all the parameters they wanted to set for her, she would have a miserable life. And they were working hard to achieve that now.

"Bottom line, guys, I don't have all the answers you want, or even any. I would like to make life better for the three foster children, and it's in my means to do so. I don't intend to adopt them. It's not my plan. Could it happen? I don't think so, but life is strange and who knows what twists or turns could occur, but I have no plan to adopt them. Xavier? He's been lovely to me. I like him. I like him a lot, and yes, he's married and getting a divorce, but not for me. He has a lovely château he rents to me. Will I date him? Probably. Will I marry him? I don't know. Will I remarry anyone? I have no idea. Is he after money? No. Will I stay in France? I don't know that either. Will I go back to Malibu? I don't know. Do I want to now? I don't. Will I continue to rent the château? I have no idea. I don't have a lot of the answers. Losing a husband is hard, and I hope it never happens to you. Having grown children who don't live in the same city is damn hard too. I'm not asking you to come home to entertain me, so don't ask me to go home when I have nothing to do there but it makes you more comfortable. That's not fair. I'll let you know if anything changes. I'm feeling my way along, and that includes Xavier. And if it weren't him, the same questions would be coming up about someone else. I'm sorry if my fostering plan upsets you, but for God's sake, at least try to be adult about it. These are kids who have suffered terrible trauma, and if I want to help them for a few months with a better life, that's entirely my business. I hope I've covered all your questions.

"I'm sorry if all of this upsets you while I try to figure

out my life. If it's too hard for you to deal with right now, go home to wherever you came from and we'll try to work it out another time. But please stop being rude to innocent children and punishing them, and being rude to my friends because they like me and I like them. They want to be nice to you, too, and they like you, God knows why, because I wouldn't like you if you treated me the way you do them. I expected you to be better than this. Thank you."

There was silence in the room after she said it, and to her credit, Lizzie was the first to apologize, and Coco was next. Justin was more hesitant, as the self-appointed head of the family.

"We just want to be sure you're with the right guy, Mom," he said, trying to justify his behavior and theirs.

"Really? Well, given the mess you've made of your life recently, you're the last person who should be making that judgment. The only thing you've done right is find Arabella, who is lovely. But you got her pregnant while you don't have a job, you can't support yourself, her, or the baby. You depend on my generosity and her father's. You didn't get married, but you got pregnant, like any sloppy fifteen-year-old in the back seat of a car. And you're getting married when she's eight months pregnant. You're about to have a baby you can't even remotely support, so as far as good judgment goes, I'm not begging or even welcoming your advice. And deciding who 'the right guy' is for me is *entirely* my business and not yours. I guess that does it," she said, annoyed with all three of them. She left the room and went to check on the children. There was silence in the room for a long time, as they looked at each other.

"She's right," Lizzie said quietly. "Her having an independent life makes us feel insecure, but it really is her business. Xavier seems like a nice guy, and the truth is those children make her happy, and she probably won't adopt them. And Xavier makes her happy too," she said fairly. Their mother had woken her up from her juvenile haze.

At that exact moment Xavier was asking Sabrina over the phone if he should come to dinner again after their blowout.

"You can if you want to," she said. "But I don't know why you'd want to. They're behaving like spoiled thirteen-year-olds. And they're not, they're ten and twelve years older."

"I'd like to come because I like them and I'd like to get to know them. It's normal that they're worried about me. They don't know me. They have no idea who I am or if I'm going to steal their mother from them. I'd like to, but there are too many of them," he said with a smile.

"I'm sorry they've been such jerks," she said apologetically. "I'm disappointed in them."

"Try not to be, they're only human. We'll try again," he said graciously. "I'm coming to dinner."

When she got off the phone with Xavier, Lizzie and Coco were playing with the children in the garden, and the children were laughing and having fun and so were her daughters. Justin was a little more miffed by what she had said. Arabella was having a rest and he was with her, complaining about his mother and how rude she had been to them, and Arabella was listening, while dozing intermittently. She slept a lot these days.

Lizzie said something important to her mother that afternoon. It had taken her years to admit it.

"You and Dad were so close and so in love that I felt shut out sometimes, and scared you didn't love me as much. And I worry sometimes now that it will happen with someone else, like Xavier."

It was a wake-up call to her mother and took her by surprise. Coco overheard Lizzie say it and sheepishly confessed that she felt that way too.

It brought tears to Sabrina's eyes and she put her arms around both her daughters and hugged them tight.

"I could never love anyone, any man, more than I do you. I loved your father but it's different. I love you, my children, more than anyone on earth." The three of them had cried and both girls looked immensely relieved. They needed to hear it from her.

*

Dinner was much better that night. Lizzie was genuinely nice to the children, Coco always had been, and they were much more civil to Xavier. Sabrina's speech got them on the right track for the rest of the week. And by the time Arabella's family came on Thursday, everyone was getting along famously.

Arabella's parents were as aristocratic as Sabrina had guessed they would be. They were fun and eccentric as only the English did so well. They had a good sense of humor, knew when to disappear, were charming and polite to everyone, and were experienced houseguests with perfect manners. And Arabella's siblings were charming and funny. Justin knew them all well. Arabella's brother flirted with Coco all weekend, and she enjoyed it. And her two pregnant sisters were funny, irreverent, and looked like twins, equally pregnant, though not as far along as their sister. And their husbands were pleasant and polite.

The wedding went off without a hitch. Everyone looked beautiful and behaved well. Xavier had provided four live musicians so they could have dancing. The children performed admirably and the grown-ups tried. The young people drank a lot, but got along. Xavier had also provided a photographer, an incredibly beautiful wedding cake, wonderful wines from his cellar, little touches Sabrina hadn't thought of. By the time the weekend was over, they all loved Xavier and said what a great guy he was, and Arabella's parents insisted that they all come to England sometime for a weekend, including the children. Sabrina had called her own children to order, and they had heard her. And they all went out on Malcolm's boat several times, in shifts because there were too many of them. It touched her heart to see the *Sabrina Fair* sailing on the ocean in Biarritz. It felt almost like Malcolm were there, and she had the feeling that he would have liked Xavier too. Justin and Arabella were well married at the end of it, with Arabella's due date only three weeks away. Sabrina was relieved, and she thought Malcolm would have been too.

On Monday after the wedding, Hallie called her. The people who wanted to rent her house in Malibu had made an offer to buy it, and Sabrina had a big decision to make. Did she want to keep the house in Malibu, and was she going back at the end of the year or not? It depended on a lot of answers she didn't know yet. She felt torn any way she turned. It was another big decision she wasn't ready to make yet. She needed more time to figure it out, but they wanted an answer, or they were going to buy another house. They were offering exactly twice what Malcolm had paid for it, which was an obscene amount of money that was hard to turn down. She didn't ask Xavier for his advice. It was her decision to make, and an emotional one only she could make.

That weekend, a week after the wedding, she left the children at the monastery, and she and Xavier spent a quiet weekend at the château alone, like grown-ups who were in love, while she was trying to decide what to do about the future. They had waited a long time for it, because of Malcolm, Brigitte, her children. They had known each other for seven months and it was perfect. They made love in what was normally his bedroom, and had been hers for the past seven months. She could feel how strong his ties to the house were. Once he was there, there was no question who it belonged to. It was his, and they had a conversation at the end of the weekend that shocked her.

They had just made love for the second time, and she turned to him with a sensual smile. She wasn't sure what to do about the house in Malibu, but she did know what she wanted to do about the château. She didn't want to give it up in January at the end of her lease. She wanted to renew the lease and stay in Arcangues, especially now, falling more and more in love with Xavier. She wasn't ready to move back to the States, whether she kept Malibu or not.

"This is an official notice," she said, snuggling up to him. "I want to renew at the end of my lease." He looked at her quietly, and stroked her hair and kissed her, and stunned her when he shook his head in answer to what she said. She thought he was teasing her, but he wasn't.

"Why not?" she asked him with wide eyes.

"For one thing, I don't need the money. I'll be getting money from the hotel by the end of the year. I was desperate in January. But it's not about the money. It's really that I want to come home. I want to be in my own house. You're not my tenant, you're the woman I love. I won't rent it again. I want to be the master of my own home." Sabrina looked crushed. "I would like to invite you to live with me here, rent-free, as the woman I love, in whatever form you wish," he said with a slow smile, and kissed her hand, then her fingers, one by one. "Is that acceptable to you?" he asked her.

"Is that a proposal?" she asked him. She wasn't ready for that yet if so. But she knew she loved him and wanted to stay in Arcangues with him.

"It's a proposal if you want it to be," he answered. "It's up to you. I'm flexible about things like that. Married or not, I love you, Sabrina. I want to live here with you until the end of my days, that's all I need to know. The rest is up to you." She loved what he had said to her. It gave her all the room she needed to be with him, and grow with him, but she still didn't know what to do about Malibu, whether to sell or not. "I think that's a question you need to ask your children, about how great an attachment they have to the house. Only they can tell you that, and what it means to them," he said when she asked his advice. She thought she could guess their answer, but she wasn't sure. Justin was making his life in London, with his career and his wife's family there. Lizzie was in love with New York, and Coco would go wherever fashion took her, probably Paris, Milan, or New York, not L.A. There was no high fashion industry in California.

Sabrina was happy living in Arcangues with Xavier. He moved in while she was still trying to decide about the house in Malibu. And he stopped her from paying him rent immediately, with him in residence with her. They got along well. It felt as though they'd always been together. She wanted to visit her gallery in L.A. from time to time and she could run it from a distance, as she had all year. She loved helping him with his gallery at the hotel. She couldn't imagine living in L.A. again. It was part of another life she had shared with Malcolm. The house in Malibu had been about them. That life was gone now. She had cherished that life and been happy, but it disappeared with Malcolm. Her life was with Xavier now. It was completely unexpected, but she was sure of it. What she didn't know about was the future, and how things would turn out.

In the end, it was easier to let the house in Malibu go than she expected. She told the children, and they agreed. The house was their history, briefly, but not their future or even their present. Their family home had been the house in Bel Air, which she and Malcolm had sold. They moved to their weekend love nest in Malibu, which had never been meant for their children. It had been her getaway with Malcolm more than theirs. Sabrina didn't need it anymore. It no longer made sense without Malcolm.

She called the realtor and accepted the offer. She told Xavier. It meant that she had no other home now, except the one she shared with him. The château belonged to him, but he made her feel at home there. Their lives had changed completely overnight. The house in Malibu faded gently from her life with no regret.

Day by day, she felt more at home at the château. And the one thing she was certain of was that Xavier was the man she loved. Their relationship and their love for each other, which neither of them could have predicted or even guessed, was the unexpected miracle that had happened when they met.

Chapter 16

There was a natural evolution to all things. September was a time of loss Sabrina knew would come. It wasn't like losing Malcolm, which was searing. It was gentler and bittersweet. The monastery had finally found Elodie and Luc's grandmother. She had been in Brittany, living with friends after the pandemic, and had recently moved back to a house of her own. She was shocked to learn she had grandchildren she didn't know. She had heard of her daughter's death in Spain but not that she had left children in France, so she had never tried to find them. She was a gentle woman, still young enough to take care of them and eager to. It was a hard day when Xavier and Sabrina took Luc and Elodie to the monastery and their grandmother was waiting for them. She promised to bring them to visit

Sabrina whenever they wanted, and Sabrina promised that she would come to see them.

The children took all their toys with them, and the clothes she'd bought them. Xavier sent their bicycles to their grandmother's home in Brittany, and Luc had just learned to ride his without the training wheels. Sabrina held the children tight for a moment and released them to their grandmother's care. It was her final act of love for them, to let them go. She cried all the way back to the château afterward. She and Xavier went out on the sailboat that afternoon and watched the sun set. She knew how much they would miss them. It was lonely for Geraldine after Elodie and Luc left. Sabrina spent extra time with her, and knew that their time together was limited and tried to prepare her for it. Sabrina wondered if Xavier's grandmother had had trouble letting them go too. But all that mattered was what was good for them and where they would be safe.

There was a rugged court case in October for Geraldine's custody. She was finally returned to her mother, which Geraldine said she wanted when the judge asked her. It was a fitting end to a traumatic year in her life. She clung to Sabrina before she left, and thanked her. She and her mother were moving to New York, where she wouldn't be hounded by her father or his relatives. Sabrina promised to visit her when she went to see Lizzie. Her bond to the three children wasn't over. It had just progressed to another place, another time. She had been there for Geraldine and Luc and Elodie when they needed her. It was a clean wound for Sabrina, and not as deep as losing Malcolm. She knew she could see them again.

"It's just us now," Xavier said when they got home. He was going to miss them too. His daughter was finally coming home for Christmas, and Sabrina's children were also coming to Arcangues. They would all be together at the château.

Xavier had started working on the renovation of a new hotel in Provence with Pascal. His divorce would be final in February. Brigitte seemed like a distant memory now. Sabrina's gentle ways had healed his scars and time was healing hers, with Xavier beside her.

She was still volunteering at the monastery and enjoyed the children. The Covid-related cases had been resolved in various ways. The number of residents at the monastery had gone back to normal, and they didn't need Sabrina and Xavier to house any children. He was the master of his château again. The hand of fate had brought them together at the right time in the right way, a good man and a good woman who needed each other to continue their journey.

*

Sabrina's children and Xavier's daughter Victoire arrived at the château on the same day in December to celebrate Christmas together. Arabella and their baby boy were there too. Lizzie and Coco hadn't seen him yet, and took turns holding him.

Sabrina smiled when she met Victoire and saw how much she looked like Xavier. She was a lovely young woman with gentle ways, and the kindness of her father. Her mother was skiing in Verbier with friends, and Victoire had wanted to spend Christmas with her father. She had a month's leave before she went back to Africa, so she had time to see her mother too. She hadn't been surprised about the divorce when Xavier told her about it and had accepted it with compassion and sympathy for him. They all knew it was right, Victoire too.

The château looked slightly different now. Sabrina had brought over her favorite pieces of furniture and art from the Malibu and Bel Air houses and they blended nicely with Xavier's ancestral pieces and gave his home a fresh new look. He loved her paintings and her taste in art. And she had left the rest in storage in L.A. for her children.

She was running both galleries, in L.A. and at the hotel, from Arcangues, and decorating Xavier and Pascal's new hotel in Provence.

The week they all spent together was heavenly chaos,

and the young people got along well, found soulmates among the group, laughed and danced and listened to the same music. They spoke a universal language of youth. Xavier and Sabrina watched them, and translated for each other when needed. Just seeing them together was a joy for them both. They had not only found each other, but their families had grown, particularly Xavier's with Sabrina's brood, and a grandchild now too, Justin's baby Theodore, Teddy. Xavier loved holding the baby and making him laugh. He was a fat, happy boy who didn't mind being passed around from hand to hand. They all had meals together and cooked together and shared good food and good wine. They had dinner at the Empress Eugénie, and went to the casino in Biarritz, and dancing afterward.

There was an abundance of joy in their lives now. Xavier took Victoire to see the mural of Noah's ark and she was awestruck by it. She and Sabrina liked each other and got along. Sabrina had the warmth and maternal instincts Victoire's own mother never had, and she soaked up Sabrina's kindness like a thirsty plant.

On Christmas morning, Sabrina had a surprise for Xavier. She had taken the old boot room no one used anymore except on very muddy days, and had turned it into a replica of the part of the original garden that Xavier loved most, minutely painted with each precise detail, every species of flower. Looking at it, you could almost smell the flowers under a cameo sky. He stood staring at it in disbelief and studied every detail, as the children looked on and smiled. They had known about the surprise for months.

"When did you do that?" he asked, pulling her close.

"When you were sleeping and at work," she said with mischief in her eyes, their children watching them, sharing their happiness.

In the mural, you could see the château in the distance, glimpsed through the trees, and a cottage with Arcangues Blue shutters. She had painted the garden on all four walls of the small, sunny room. It was her gift to him, as their life together was to each other, a rainbow of colors, each one more beautiful than the next. He knew what her words meant now, like their life together since they met, and the lessons they had learned from each other and the strength they shared. The room she had painted for him was the color of hope.

Danielle Steel

Have you liked Danielle Steel on Facebook?

Be the first to know about Danielle's latest books, access exclusive competitions and stay in touch with news about Danielle.

www.facebook.com/DanielleSteelOfficial

THE DEVIL'S DAUGHTER

The face of evil.

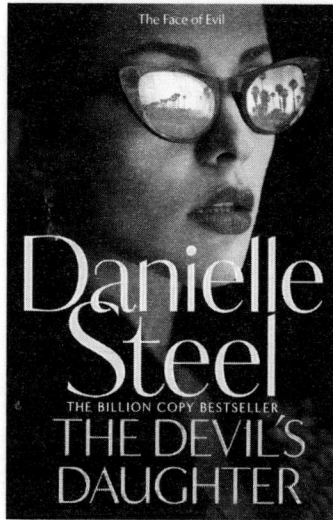

Billie and Mickie Banks grew up on a small farm in the American Midwest. As sisters, they couldn't be more different. Determined to seek fame and fortune, Mickie moves to LA and becomes involved with Alex Addison, a smooth-talking but unscrupulous surgeon. Billie grows suspicious of the mystery around Mickie's new life and the person she's involved with, but her concern for her sister is met with contempt. Just as Mickie discovers the life of wealth and extravagance she's always craved, a major scandal threatens to blow her world apart. As Mickie risks a prison sentence, Billie must ask herself whether bad people can ever truly change.

ABOUT THE AUTHOR

DANIELLE STEEL has been hailed as one of the world's most popular authors, with a billion copies of her novels sold. Her many international bestsellers include *The Portrait, For Richer for Poorer* and *A Mother's Love*. She is also the author of *His Bright Light*, the story of her son Nick Traina's life and death; *A Gift of Hope,* a memoir of her work with the homeless; and the children's books *Pretty Minnie in Paris* and *Pretty Minnie in Hollywood*. Danielle divides her time between Paris and her home in northern California.

daniellesteel.com
Facebook.com/DanielleSteelOfficial
Instagram: @officialdaniellesteel